MY HIGHLAND CAPTOR

Warriors of the Highlands, Book 3

MIRIAM MINGER

OLIVER
HEBER
BOOKS

PUBLISHER'S NOTE: This is a work of fiction. Names, characters, places, and incidents either are the product of the author's imagination or are used fictitiously. Any resemblance to actual persons, living or dead, business establishments, events, or locales is entirely coincidental.

COPYRIGHT © Miriam Minger

Published by Oliver-Heber Books

0 9 8 7 6 5 4 3 2 1

SERIES BIBLIOGRAPHY

Warriors of the Highlands

My Highland Warrior

My Highland Protector

My Highland Captor

My Highland Raider

My Highland Champion

CHAPTER 1

DUMBARTON CASTLE,
DUMBARTONSHIRE, SCOTLAND, 1307

"Forgive me, my lord king, *but I dinna want a bride*!"

Conall Campbell had no more than entered the antechamber when his vehement protest burst from him, the same words that had echoed in his brain from the moment a messenger had arrived at Campbell Castle three days ago with a summons from King Robert.

A summons stating that the king might have found a bride for him and to ride straightaway to Dumbarton to discuss the matter, and Conall had reluctantly obeyed.

The entire journey a torment. Each passing league like a noose tightening around his neck.

Now he had voiced his pent-up objection, yet he felt no relief at the immediate darkening of King Robert's expression, which did not bode well for their meeting.

Och, not at all. Drawing a deep breath, Conall planted his feet and stood at attention as the king approached him, though his heart still thundered in protest.

King Robert wasn't as tall as Conall—aye, few men were taller, other than his older brother Cameron and their longtime friend and former commander, Gabriel

MacLachlan—but he cut an imposing figure, nonetheless, with his muscular physique and air of authority.

An authority that Conall had challenged the moment he had entered the room leading into the great hall of Dumbarton Castle, God forgive him.

He might have helped to save Robert the Bruce's life some weeks ago, but that did not give him the right to overstep his overlord and king. As King Robert's light brown eyes bored into his own, Conall swallowed hard but did not allow his gaze to falter.

"What are you, Conall Campbell? A petulant youth tae greet me with such an outburst? Where is your sense of discipline?"

Conall had no answer, for he was convicted by his rashness. He could just hear Cameron's rebuke if his brother had witnessed such a display, reminding him as he'd done since Conall's boyhood to think before he spoke—or acted. Yet the fact remained, a tic working along the hard set of Conall's jaw. *He wanted no bride*!

"You're a wild one, Campbell...only your usually good-natured temperament sparing you a reputation as a seducer of the worst kind. Did you think for a moment that I'm not aware of your exploits with women? I can imagine a wife for you might seem a terrible prospect, aye, a burdensome yoke around your neck. A hindrance tae the wanton life you wish tae lead. Yet the time has come for me tae reward you for helping tae save my life, and your marriage is part of that plan."

"I need no reward, my lord king," Conall interjected, feeling somewhat unsettled by King Robert's blunt—yet accurate—assessment of him. "Serving you is honor enough, my loyalty unwavering—"

"Good, so now you'll have a chance tae prove your allegiance. I want revenge for the deaths earlier this year of my brothers Alexander and Thomas, and you're the man tae help me accomplish it."

Conall could only stare at him, wholly taken by surprise.

He knew of the sea invasion in February against King Edward's forces that had gone terribly awry, with Alexander and Thomas Bruce's men slaughtered and the brothers taken prisoner and executed in Carlisle.

A grisly death, the two of them hung, drawn, and beheaded. King Robert was no doubt thinking the same thing, for his scowl had deepened as he held Conall's gaze.

"Your fame as a fearsome warrior is matched only by a few—your brother Cameron among them—though you're also known for daring on the battlefield that borders on foolhardiness. You're quick-witted and fleet of foot, and as strong as three men when caught in a fight. All qualities that will serve you well when you steal Euan MacCulloch's intended bride right from under his nose. I hold *him* most responsible for my brothers' capture and death—and for this offense, he will pay."

"Steal his bride, King Robert?" Conall echoed. "Wouldna it be easier for me tae find the bastard and cut his throat?"

"Easier, aye, but too quick a punishment for his unforgiveable crime against my family. He'll suffer in ways large and small until I drive him and all of his kinsmen from Scotland—starting with the abduction of his bride, Isabeau Charpentier."

Conall could tell from the angry bitterness in the king's voice that there would be no swaying him, which meant his fate was all but sealed.

A Frenchwoman no less, from the sound of her name, King Edward's court filled with such arranged marriages between his long-time foes in France and his loyal supporters at home, English and Scots alike. How better to maintain a fragile peace?

Yet now Edward had died earlier in the month, his weakling son, another Edward, on the throne. The new king's wife, Isabella, was a Frenchwoman as well—och, what did any of this matter? Conall wanted no bride of any ilk!

"You would force this woman upon me?" Conall asked with quiet bluntness. "This...Isabeau Charpentier? She will hate me. Make my life a misery—"

"Or you will charm her as you've done tae many before her," King Robert cut him off, his tone as blunt. "It's time for you tae think of the future, a wife and family. An estate a few hours' ride from Campbell Castle will await you upon your return, with extensive lands and a castle by the sea, and your own forces tae command. The place has only recently been cleared of its MacDougall inhabitants, but that has been my charge tae your brother and Gabriel MacLachlan and you all along. While I fight tae subdue any resistance among Scots nobles tae my rule, you will remain in Argyll tae prevent Clan MacDougall from regaining power. A straightforward and worthy task, aye?"

Conall nodded, for he could do naught but agree.

King Robert had spoken. Conall had never yearned for a great estate, but one was being offered to him and he could not refuse.

Yet wife or no, he fully intended to go on as he had before, for *no* woman would ever rule his heart.

Unbeknownst even to his brother, he had given his love only once and it had been hurled back in his face. Never again would he suffer such humiliation, such pain. *Never*.

"Do you accept my plan for you, Conall?"

"Aye."

"Good, then we've reached an understanding. Abduct her, wed her, and bed her before you return tae introduce me tae your new bride. I've full confidence that you'll use every amorous weapon in your arsenal tae accomplish your mission—and my revenge against the MacCullochs will have finally begun. You'll find your bride lodged at a convent just outside Dumfries until the wedding on Sunday. It's tae be a grand affair, or so my spies tell me. I'd give anything tae see the look on Euan MacCulloch's face when he discovers the beauteous Isabeau has been snatched away from him."

"Beauteous, my lord king?"

"Aye, as lissome and lovely as they come, if that's any consolation tae you. Dark hair, dark eyes, skin like alabaster..." Now King Robert's expression held a flicker of amusement as he gave a short laugh. "You're incorrigible, Campbell, the perfect man for the task. I almost pity the lass—och, enough. Will you join me for supper? The morning and a long ride south will arrive before you know it."

The king brushed past him as if not expecting an answer. Conall could but turn and stride after him from the antechamber into the great hall crowded with courtiers, warriors, and sundry others as servants rushed between tables filling ale cups.

Ale. Just what he needed. He planned to drink a barrel of it.

Anything to dull the realization that his life would never be the same in a few days' time.

A bride. A *French* bride. Would she even speak Gaelic? Probably so, if she had been pledged to a Scotsman.

"A dozen of my men, as well as those that rode here with you, will accompany you as close tae Dumfries as it's safe for them tae travel," King Robert said over his shoulder as he climbed the steps to the dais, gesturing for Conall to accompany him. "Since Edward regained the town last year, it's overrun with Scots loyal tae England. One day I vow Dumfries will fall again tae my forces—but for now you'll be on your own while looking for your bride."

"On my own..." Conall said under his breath, taking

the empty seat beside King Robert at the long trestle table where his closest advisors already sat.

"Aye. It's better that way. You'll draw less attention tae yourself. No one will suspect such an audacious act, but a disguise of some sort is probably in order. Mayhap a friar—och, but then you'd have tae trim that midnight hair."

Conall sighed heavily, more eager than ever to drain his first cup of ale as the king snorted out a laugh.

"Your good humor seems tae have fled, Conall— och, I dinna blame you. It's a dangerous mission and you might not survive it...though something tells me that you will. Ah, yes, a priest will also accompany you, Father Titus, and wait for you with the others. He'll perform the wedding when you meet up with them again. Find a church so you can record the marriage, but dinna delay the ceremony even if she fights you."

"God help me," Conall muttered, that prospect as unappetizing as the platters of roasted meat being placed before them.

He didn't want food, just strong drink and lots of it. A buxom serving maid with dark brown curls hastened to fill his cup, her creamy breasts nearly spilling from her bodice as she bent low before him.

"Is there anything else I can do for you?" she queried with a saucy smile, though King Robert waved her away before Conall could answer.

"Dinna you ever tire of it, man? Women swarming around you like flies tae honey? You didna say even a word tae her and she was ready tae jump onto your lap!"

Conall shrugged, for even the lasses seemed to hold no interest for him tonight. He found himself thinking about the one that had spurned him four years ago with her honey-gold hair and flashing green eyes, which only made him clasp his cup tightly and drain the ale with one long swallow.

He had sworn to himself never to think of Lorna,

for she had wed a brawny blacksmith only days after telling him that the last thing she wanted was to marry a warrior.

"You'll only die in battle one day—and then where will that leave me? Alone and probably with a mewling babe at my breast and another wee bairn at my feet, and no coin for food or even a roof over our head."

Och, he had been only eighteen, and certain that he had found the love of his life, only for her to say that she had enjoyed their time together, aye, especially their lovemaking, but she was done with him. Cameron had been gone on a campaign with their overlord, Earl Seoras, the entire two months Conall had wooed her, and he had never once mentioned her after his brother returned—though Cameron had queried him in vain about his sullen demeanor.

Love of his life? Conall laughed wryly under his breath, though he could not deny that the pain of her betrayal lingered still no matter the beds he had shared since.

Outwardly, he was all lighthearted teasing, kisses, and caresses with the lasses, deceiving his brother and all others around him—aye, better that than to reveal he had been such a fool when it came to love. Another serving maid ventured near, her light-colored hair glistening like gold in the torchlight...like honey...and this time he smiled back at her when she bent over to refill his cup.

A warm, engaging smile he'd used so many times that always seemed to bring a heated blush to fair cheeks and a returned smile that showed an eager willingness for whatever else he might have in mind.

"Och, Campbell, I've never seen the like," King Robert mused as his own cup was refilled. "I canna imagine being born as handsome and strapping a man as you—but I've done well for myself all the same, aye?"

Conall nodded in deference, sensing a deep loneliness in the middle-aged man seated beside him for a beloved and much younger wife that had been taken prisoner last year by the English, and whom he had no idea if he would ever see again.

Aye, if King Robert wanted revenge against the Scots enemies who sided with England against their own kind, Conall would oblige him with no further objections. No more outbursts. No drowning his dismay in ale or in the arms of a willing woman, though the idea of taking a wife still chafed him.

His loyalty to his king and a free and independent Scotland mattered above all else.

"A friar, my lord king?" Conall queried, forcing a smile and hoping to draw King Robert from the melancholy that seemed to have drifted over him no matter the raucous mood in the hall. "I was thinking mayhap a friar *and* a healer. They're always needed and can gain admittance tae any household if one appears with a basket of vials and potions. Do you think your own healers might loan me some supplies tae help me pass for one of their own?"

The king lowered his cup to study him for a moment, almost looking relieved that Conall appeared to have accepted what lay in front of him, and then gave a nod.

"Quick-witted, just as I said—and as daring as they come. Aye, Campbell, whatever you need, it's yours."

CHAPTER 2

CONVENT OF THE GREY FRIARS,
DUMFRIES, SCOTLAND

"**Y**ou clumsy fool, will you yank the hair from my scalp? Give me that comb, I'll do it myself!"

Lisette gasped as her irate half-sister, Isabeau Charpentier, snatched the ivory comb from her and struck her with it, leaving a red mark on the back of her hand.

Wincing in pain, Lisette stepped back just in time to avoid another blow, which made Isabeau utter a high-pitched squeal of rage. Her beautiful face contorted and with her long dark hair whirling around her, she jumped up from the chair and advanced upon Lisette.

"Get out, you're of no use to me at all! Why did I ever bring you with me from France? I should have cast you out onto the street like my sainted mother bade me right before she died, but no. Out of the goodness of my heart, I kept you on as my lady's maid, which is more than your incompetence deserves. *Get out!*"

Lisette didn't waste another moment in obliging her. She fled across the room and flung open the door just as the comb hit the doorjamb, barely missing her head.

"Lord help us," breathed a young nun who stood stock-still and wide-eyed in the hallway, holding a breakfast tray. "Is she always so out of sorts in the morning? Here, *you* take the tray. I dinna dare go in there."

9

Lisette had only just closed the door behind her before she had the tray thrust into her hands, the nun not waiting for any explanation but crossing herself and scurrying back down the hall.

Lisette wanted to cross herself, too, but she would have dropped the tray. Instead, she moved to one side of the door and leaned against the wall, tears smarting her eyes though she swallowed hard to force them back.

Tears were useless. She had learned that well enough since her father, Hugh Charpentier, had died a year ago and left her at the mercy of Isabeau and her equally mean-spirited mother, Claudia, who had gone to her grave only two months past.

How desperately Lisette wished she had remained in France instead of traveling by ship to Dumfries, Scotland, with a half-sister who had been taught since infancy to hate her! A half-sister who would be wed in two days to a Scotsman, Euan MacCulloch, who couldn't wait to sink his teeth into her fortune, a fair sum of which should have gone to Lisette, as Hugh's illegitimate younger daughter.

Yet her poor father, at the height of his delirium brought on by a deadly fever, had signed a new will that had bequeathed everything to Claudia—his lands in Normandy, his castle—and all had been inherited by Isabeau upon her mother's death. Not a single coin had been left for Lisette after Hugh had tried to provide for her, she sensed as much out of love as of guilt for the misery she had suffered from years of Claudia and Isabeau's abuse.

He had done his best to protect her by giving Lisette his surname, but his domineering wife had made his life a misery as well for fathering a bastard that had been foisted upon her after Lisette's mother had died in childbirth.

A kitchen maid, no less...Elise.

All Lisette knew of her from servants forbidden by

Claudia to ever speak of her was that her mother had been as sweet-tempered as a fawn and as lovely a young woman as they had seen with mahogany-colored hair and soft brown eyes...just like Lisette.

The little she had gleaned about her mother had given her some comfort over the years, and helped to hold back despair, but now fresh tears welled again at the fate Isabeau had in store for her. A fate Isabeau had taunted her with again that morning...

"I cannot have you stay within my household and risk you turning the head of my husband like your whore of a mother did to my father."

"*Our* father, you mean," Lisette had said under her breath in a rare show of dissent, for she had learned a year ago that speaking up for herself only brought added misery.

Slaps to her face when she least expected it.

Her food delivered cold to her sparsely furnished room on an upper floor of the castle they had left behind in Normandy...if it came at all.

Unseasoned logs in the small fireplace that smoked more than burned and offered her little warmth.

Servants forbidden to speak to her or to assist her.

Claudia and Isabeau's cruel offenses had not been so blatant while Hugh had been alive, but after his death—

"Lisette, where *are* you?"

She had jumped at the door flung open, Isabeau stepping out into the hall and lifting her chin imperiously.

"Ah, so my breakfast tray has come. Why are you dallying? Will you leave me in this room to starve?"

Lisette shook her head and followed Isabeau back into the plainly furnished bedchamber, the blue silk of her half-sister's gown swishing around her legs while Lisette's scratchy woolen tunic chafed hers.

All of her lovely clothes had been taken away at her father's death, and she had been made to dress like the lowliest of servant girls, her garments ill-fitting and coarse.

Her few pieces of jewelry were gone, too, a gold ring set with a perfectly rounded pearl that her father had presented to her for her seventeenth birthday just before he died. His precious gift had disappeared one day from her bedside table and she hadn't seen it since.

The other was a necklace with a delicate gold cross that her father had given to her mother, which Elise had been wearing when she died, Hugh holding her lifeless hand and weeping at her bedside. The family's old healer had told Lisette as much when she was old enough to understand, mayhap wanting her to know that her father had borne a great love for her mother.

When Claudia had gotten wind of it from a servant who had overheard the healer's words, she had banished the man from ever stepping foot in the castle again. Yet Hugh had refused to allow his wife to take the necklace from Lisette, which he had given to her when she was only six years old.

Lisette would never forget how Claudia had snatched the cross from her neck the very moment her father had breathed his last, and cast it into the crackling flames in the fireplace.

A terrible thing to do. An unholy thing, Claudia's triumphant expression and the hatred glittering in her dark eyes a foreshadowing of abuse to come.

Lisette had thought a hundred times of running away, but where?

She had no coin to her name. No other family. That kind healer had long ago gone to his grave. Now she was in a foreign land with Isabeau planning to wed her to one of the brutish warriors that had accompanied Laird MacCulloch to meet their ship—for so she had threatened moments ago, making Lisette's hand slip with the comb.

Her hands begun to shake again at the thought,

Lisette set the tray on the table next to the chair where Isabeau had plopped down, though her half-sister made no move to serve herself.

"Hand me that bowl, Lisette—God help us, do these nuns eat nothing but porridge for breakfast? No sweet pastries? No jam? If it's the same at my new husband's castle, my plan to marry you off as soon as I'm wed won't be the only change I make—"

"Leave me here at the convent, I don't wish to wed one of those men," Lisette broke in with a small wince, wondering what Isabeau might hurl at her now. The bowl? Her half-sister stared at her as if she couldn't believe Lisette had dared to speak up, but to Lisette's surprise, Isabeau merely shrugged and dug her spoon into the porridge.

"What you want is of no consequence, you silly chit. Do you think it was *my* choice to come to Scotland for a husband? My marriage to Laird MacCulloch is just another alliance arranged by King Edward to secure ties between England and France, no matter he's dead now and his son on the throne. At least Euan is pleasing to look upon and not some gaseous old man fumbling at me on our wedding night—*mon Dieu!*" Isabeau spat out the porridge and wiped her mouth with the back of her hand. "This foul stuff is tasteless! I wish I could wed this very hour and not wait until Sunday, if only to leave this place and enjoy some decent food. Get it out of my sight!"

Lisette obliged her...anything to avoid the bowl thrown at her head. She had barely picked up the tray and moved it to a table near the narrow window when Isabeau launched herself from the chair.

"I almost forgot, Euan will be here soon to take me to visit the church so I can see it before we're wed. He said it would be filled with wildflowers for our wedding. Isn't that thoughtful of him? Fetch a cloak for me, Lisette, so I can go await him in the courtyard."

Accustomed to having orders barked at her, she nodded and threw open one of the three large chests Isabeau had brought with her from France—each filled to the brim with fine garments in silk and satin, matching slippers, and luxurious fur-trimmed cloaks. Lisette pulled out the dark blue one on top and rushed over to Isabeau, who snatched it out of her hand and whirled it around her shoulders.

"How do I look? Will my future husband be pleased?"

"*Oui*, you look beautiful, Isabeau."

In all honesty, how could Lisette say otherwise? Her half-sister's stunning beauty had the effect of making most men stop cold to stare at her, and so had Laird MacCulloch upon his first glimpse of his bride when Isabeau had disembarked from the ship almost two weeks ago. Few women were comelier, though Lisette had noticed appraising looks cast her way, too, in spite of her plain brown tunic and tightly braided hair.

The two of them clearly were sisters for how much they resembled each other, both with willowy figures and creamy skin, though Lisette was shorter and her waist-length brown hair tinged with reddish highlights. She and Isabeau had both just turned eighteen, too, Lisette only a few weeks younger. For a fleeting moment, she saw that Isabeau's expression had softened at her compliment, but then a sneer marred her half-sister's lovely features.

"Don't think that your pretty praise will spare you from my plans for you. Enjoy the peace of this wretched convent while you can, and you'd do well to eat that porridge. From the look of these Scotsmen, they're a lusty lot. We can't have you disappointing your brawny new husband on your wedding night."

Isabeau's amused laughter followed her from the room and down the hallway, leaving Lisette to sink into the nearest chair in despair.

The cloying scent of Isabeau's lilac perfume hung in the air, which only made Lisette feel like retching as she stared at the now cold bowl of porridge.

A husband from among Laird MacCulloch's men... and not a kind-looking face among them. How would he treat her? No doubt like a servant as had Claudia and Isabeau, but with the carnal use of her body thrown in to terrify her.

In her heart of hearts, she had dreamed of marrying one day...a good man, an honorable man like her father. Yet even with his strength of character, he hadn't been strong enough to prevent Claudia's cruelty towards her, Lisette certain that when her mother had died, he had lost a part of himself with her.

What must it be like to know such a profound love that the loss of it would cause enduring sorrow and heartache? Her father had always seemed to her to have one foot in life and the other in the grave, as if he couldn't wait to see his beloved Elise again.

Sighing, Lisette rose from the chair and went to the tray to take a few bites of porridge, if only to ease the noisy pangs in her stomach.

Isabeau had been right, it was tasteless, but what else was she to do?

She must eat. She must live...and she refused to give up hope that angels in heaven would light another path for her.

A desperate thought, but mayhap she could plead with Laird MacCulloch to allow her to stay at the convent, which would give her some time to come up with another plan. No doubt her even approaching the Scotsman would enrage Isabeau, but what didn't upset her half-sister when it had anything to do with Lisette?

Sighing more plaintively, she set down the bowl and began to tidy up the room, a streak of sunlight falling upon the shimmering pale pink satin of Isabeau's wedding gown in the open trunk.

Such a beautiful garment...while the coarse wool of Lisette's tunic suddenly seemed to chafe her all the more.

Isabeau was most likely gone for a few hours to visit the church, yes? What would be the harm if Lisette enjoyed the silky comfort of such fabric against her skin—even if only for a few moments? *Dare she?*

Her heart beating faster, Lisette ran to the door to close it, and then turned back into the room that now seemed awash in golden light streaming from the window.

As if drawn by some unseen hand, she went to the chest and pulled out the wedding gown and laid it upon Isabeau's bed.

A goose down mattress piled with soft blankets while her cot with its one thin blanket was pushed up against an opposite wall—no, no, she wouldn't think right now of her half-sister's multitude of unkindnesses and simmering jealousies!

Lisette wanted to pretend that the exquisite wedding gown was for her as she prepared to marry a man who truly loved her. A man who would never hurt her. A man who would do anything to protect and cherish her—ah, please, God, was there such a one walking the earth?

Her hands trembled as she quickly pulled her tunic over her head, tossing it to the floor, and then let the silken gown drift down over her like a gossamer pink cloud.

She wasn't surprised at all that the garment fit her perfectly, other than being a bit too long, and she kicked off her worn leather slippers to let the cool fabric tickle her toes.

With shaking fingers she loosed her thick, waist-length hair from its braid, freshly washed last night in a basin of cold water after Isabeau had gone to sleep, and let it cascade down her back.

The sheer freedom of the moment overwhelmed her and made her twirl around in the middle of the room as Lisette laughed with delight.

She spun and spun, closing her eyes, her arms outstretched, until she felt lightheaded from the sheer joy of it and stopped to sink to her knees.

Breathless, she heard only her heartbeat pounding in her ears, her breasts rising and falling...until she froze in the next instant when she felt a draft as if the door was open.

Ah, God, no, *Isabeau*!

Bracing for a shriek of outrage, Lisette opened her eyes and lifted her head, only to gasp at the sight of a looming figure a few feet away from her.

Not Isabeau at all...but the tallest, most strapping friar she had ever seen in her life, reaching out his hand to her.

"Get up, woman—and dinna utter a sound or you'll bring the whole convent down upon us. Do you understand me?"

CHAPTER 3

Did *she understand him?*
     She nodded, his Gaelic accent as thick as any she'd heard since arriving in Scotland, though she gasped again when he leaned down and pulled her to her feet.

None too gently, either, which suddenly filled her with alarm.

He was dressed in a dark gray habit from his hooded head to his leather shoes, but the woolen garment looked to be straining at the seams, the man was so big. She couldn't fully see his face, either, but when she tried to break free of him, his vehement curse made her knees grow weak.

A curse? The man was no more a friar than she was a blushing bride-to-be! Lisette began to struggle in earnest, which only made the giant Scotsman clutch her all the more tightly, his tone grown exasperated as he clapped a huge hand over her mouth.

"Och, I was a fool tae think you wouldna fight me!"

Terror gripping her, Lisette saw him fumble with his free hand in a basket full of vials and bottles slung over his arm, until he grabbed one and pulled out the cork stopper with his teeth.

The next thing Lisette knew, he tilted the open vial

into her mouth, a foul-tasting syrup going down her throat that made her cough and sputter.

"Forgive me, lass, but there was no help for it. I willna hurt you, I vow it. You'll be fast asleep in a few moments—aye, it would have been easier if you hadna fought me, but I dinna blame you at all. Och, there she goes."

The last words were out of her captor's mouth at the same moment Lisette felt a strange warmth coursing through her that made her limbs go weak and her head to loll to one side.

Dear God, what was happening to her?

Lisette heard the man grunt with exertion as, through dimming eyes, she watched him grab from the trunk a burgundy-colored cloak made especially to complement Isabeau's wedding gown, and wrap her in it from head to foot. Then she was the one to grunt as he hoisted her so abruptly over his shoulder that the breath was knocked from her body, everything around her growing black.

As if from a deep well, she heard the door opened wider, and then the sensation of her captor running as her head bounced against his broad back.

It was the last thing she felt...a high-pitched female scream followed by another fierce curse, the last thing she heard.

Conall lunged past the startled nun who stood with her hand to her throat, muttering, "Forgive me, Sister," as he kicked open the main door to the convent's sleeping quarters.

Damn it all, he had hoped to get in and get out without anyone seeing him, but the older woman had stepped from her room into the hallway just as he passed by with his unconscious load slung over his shoulder.

He should have thought of something clever to explain his presence—he'd been summoned to look in on Lady Isabeau Charpentier, who was suffering from a headache, or some such excuse—but what of his cloak-wrapped bundle? How would he explain that away? It was just as well that he hoist up his friar's habit and run like hell toward the high stone wall enclosing the convent, where a pretty novice waited for him.

Aye, thinking of hell, if he hadn't been destined for Satan's fiery pit already, he surely was now after cajoling the young nun-in-training to unbolt a weathered door set into the wall for him.

No more than a few moments ago, he had stood on the strong back of his horse to peer over the wall when the novice had been walking by on her way to morning prayers at the chapel—or so she had told him.

He had decided as soon as he reached the convent that he would waste no time in trying to talk his way into gaining entrance through the main gate, but would go around to the back that was nearer to the sleeping quarters. To his relief, the layout of the place was much like the convent outside Dumbarton where Gabriel MacLachlan had gone to fetch his bride two months ago, both Conall and Cameron accompanying him—which had made Conall's task so much easier in finding Isabeau Charpentier.

That, and cajoling the pretty novice to open the creaky door so he wouldn't have to climb over the wall...and there she still stood, just where he had left her, as wide-eyed and trusting as a spring lamb as he drew closer, slowing his pace.

"I heard a scream, Friar."

"It was nothing," Conall said with a glance over his shoulder, but thankfully no alarm had been raised. Had that older nun been so stunned that she still stood rooted to the floor? Shrugging, he hoped so. "I found Lady Isabeau's chamber just where you'd said...three doors down on the left. She's very ill, though, so I must take her into town where another healer has much more knowledge of such matters."

The novice nodded, her fair brow crinkling with concern. "Oh, aye, Friar, please hurry. She's tae be married in two days. Shall I tell the Reverend Mother that you'll bring her back soon?"

"Aye, you do that," Conall replied with a deep twinge of guilt. He hoped the novice, mayhap no more than fifteen years old, would not suffer any unpleasant consequences for so innocently helping him. He made the sign of the Cross over her and then ducked through the door. "Dinna forget tae draw the door and then on with you tae your prayers."

"God go with you, Friar, and the beautiful lady."

Aye, he was bound straight for hell, Conall thought grimly as the novice shut the door with a thud and drew the bolt just as he'd bade her.

It had all been so easy...too easy, but mayhap that was soon to change. The hair prickled on the back of his neck at the distant sound of riders approaching. He untethered his roan stallion from a tree stump and hoisted himself into the saddle, his unconscious burden still slung over his shoulder and the basket filled with clinking bottles over his arm.

What a strange sight he must be! As the thunder of hooves drew closer, Conall urged his horse into a gallop and rode straight for a thick copse of trees, where he pulled up on the reins and took cover just in time.

Three men headed straight for the main gate of the convent, one riding in front and the other two behind, but their pace wasn't rushed as if there was anything amiss.

Instead the dark-haired warrior, who appeared to be the leader, threw back his head and laughed at something said by one of the others, all of them in high spirits—and then it dawned upon Conall.

Surely the one in front must be Euan MacCulloch coming to visit his bride-to-be, which made Conall curse under his breath and urge his horse deeper into the trees.

A bride-to-be that was sleeping like the dead, her dark hair streaming down his back and her slight weight no more a nuisance to him than if he'd had a child thrown over his shoulder. He lowered her to his lap all the same so he could better hold onto her, and then shook off the basket from his arm.

It occurred to him as the vials and bottles spilled onto the mossy ground that he might have had cause to use some of those healer's potions during the journey back to Dumbarton Castle, but there was no help for it now. When MacCulloch realized his bride-to-be was missing, an alarm would be raised and a frantic search begun, which made Conall kick his horse into a hard gallop.

He had left the rest of his men and the priest that had accompanied them some ten leagues to the north. It wouldn't take long for him to reach them, but then they would have to ride at a breakneck pace from that point to elude any searchers that might be sent out in all directions from Dumfries.

Aye, and a fruitless search it would be, too, for Euan MacCulloch would never see his intended bride again.

Conall had her now, and though it grated upon him mightily that he must marry her, he felt a heady sense of triumph to have abducted her with so little trouble at all—and won King Robert a goodly measure of revenge.

How pleased the man would be! Yet Conall's full task wasn't yet accomplished, for he still had to wed and bed her.

"Och, easier thought of than done," he muttered,

scowling now though he tightened his arms around his captive as he glanced down at her upturned face pressed against his chest.

Isabeau Charpentier.

Now *his* intended bride. King Robert's description of her as beauteous hardly did her justice, for in truth, Conall doubted he had ever seen a lovelier young woman. His first sight of her had nearly undone him, his loins tightening as much at the vivid memory as that her softly rounded rump was wedged between his thighs.

Aye, he could indulge in such thoughts now that he had ridden well away from the convent, though he didn't allow his charging stallion to slacken their pace.

He would never have imagined finding the woman he was sent to abduct twirling around in her room with her slender arms outstretched and her lilting laughter filling the air.

He had quietly pushed open the door to her chamber, expecting to find her still abed and asleep—but no, not this one. He had stood there for a moment like a dolt, mesmerized by the sight of her, aye, and with the sweet smell of her lilac perfume arousing his senses.

Her lissome figure awash in sunlight beneath a pale pink gown that hugged every tempting curve, her long dark hair tinged with red that had startled him...like glimmering streaks of fire.

Yet it had been her face filled with such joy that had most struck him, her eyes closed, her head tilted back, her rose-pink lips curved into a smile that made him feel like a brute to have come to steal her away from whatever had made her so happy.

Her upcoming marriage? Euan MacCulloch? Mayhap upon first sight of her future husband, she had fallen deeply in love—och, what did it matter?

The thing was done, the spell broken when Isabeau

had sunk to her knees, clearly to catch her breath, and Conall had stepped further into the room.

She had appeared to freeze as if sensing his presence, her expression no longer one of joy but of sheer dread.

Only then had she opened her eyes to look up at him, his breath catching at their soft brown hue—aye, he couldn't deny it, while the dismay emanating from her had instantly become confusion.

Yet why wouldn't she have appeared confused to find a man dressed as a friar standing in her bedchamber? A confusion that had all too quickly become alarm and then panic, Conall grateful for the sleeping elixir that he had forced down her throat.

Isabeau had understood him, that much he knew, for she had nodded when he spoke to her in Gaelic, which was something else to be grateful for. He knew a wee bit of the French language, but not enough to explain to her what had occurred—and what *else* would soon occur—as soon as she regained consciousness.

A ragged sigh rose to Conall above the pounding of his horse's hooves, which made him slow his mount's pace since he judged they were far enough from the convent now to warrant it.

Yet still she slept within his arms, though in the sunlight he saw a wetness streaking her face that startled him.

Tears?

He held the reins with one hand and touched her cheek, her skin warm to the touch as his fingertip came away wet.

Was she caught in some nightmare? Was there some foul ingredient in the potion he'd given her that was making frightening phantoms inhabit her mind?

Hugging her closer, Conall felt sickened that he might have made her suffer such an ill effect, but there was nothing to be done about it.

All he could do was keep riding while hoping that the men who had accompanied him had managed to stay hidden from any passing English soldiers or Scotsmen loyal to their enemies to the south.

Mayhap by the time he rejoined them, Isabeau would be awake and he could apprise her of her fate. At once he envisioned screams and struggles and attempts to escape and more tears, which made Conall swear to himself and shake his head.

"Och, man, why the devil did you discard that basket? Now you've nothing left tae calm the lass, no matter it gives her bad dreams."

At the sound of his voice, his horse snorted and tossed his head as if agreeing with him, and now Conall laughed, though he felt little humor.

Here he was riding north toward the Highlands with a woman he had no wish to marry, and who would most likely hate him for the rest of his life for stealing her from the man she loved and the life she'd envisioned for herself—God help him!

What a pair made in heaven.

~

"She's gone."

Isabeau had breathed the obvious as she stood beside Euan MacCulloch in the bedchamber she had left no more than a half hour ago.

No signs of a struggle at all, only Lisette's woolen tunic upon the floor, which made Isabeau's gaze flit to the open trunk that looked as if someone had rummaged through it.

"Ah, *non*, my beautiful wedding gown is gone, too!"

She ran to the trunk and stared in horror while Sister Damaris, the Reverend Mother of the convent, stood in the doorway and wrung her bony hands.

"Please dinna blame our young novice, it wasna her

fault! The friar said he was a healer come tae tend tae Lady Isabeau and that no one had answered his knock at the main gate, so the child opened the door in the back wall for him. She was only trying tae help. Then he left a few moments later with the lady slung over his shoulder—God be praised that it wasn't you, Lady Isabeau!"

"Aye, a foul plot was afoot here," interjected Euan, his ruddy face flushed and his hazel eyes filled with fury. "The man didna come here tae abduct a lady's maid, but tae steal my bride. She must have dressed herself in your wedding gown for her own amusement, Isabeau, what other explanation can there be? The fiend thought the lass was you, which is no surprise. She looks just like you with her dark hair and face like an angel—"

"*Angel?*" Isabeau cut him off, though what did it matter now if Euan had thought Lisette fair to look upon?

She was gone! A godsend! A miracle, for Lisette was finally out of her life and no more did she need concern herself with her half-sister turning her new husband's head. Yet a closer look at the trunk made her stomach turn and her knees suddenly feel weak as she pushed aside several garments, searching...

No, no, it couldn't be! The burgundy cloak she'd had made especially from the finest and softest wool was gone, too—and with it a fortune in jewels that had been sewn into the hem.

Jewels that her mother, Claudia, had bought with the sale of some of their lands, a transaction that Isabeau had no intention of sharing with Euan. Claudia had sworn her to secrecy, her words flying back to Isabeau...

"One cannot say what life will bring to you, my darling daughter. With your marriage, Euan will be the master of your inheritance, but at least with these jewels, you will never be dependent upon any man. Guard them well!"

Guard them well...

Feeling as if she might retch, Isabeau spun to face Euan and did her best to force convincing tears to her eyes. "You must find her, Euan! I haven't told you the truth because of the shame to our family, but Lisette is my half-sister. A bastard half-sister that my father brought into our home when she was just a babe, at my mother's kind insistence. We've always done our best to do right by her and we grew to love her so. We can't just leave her to this wretched abductor!"

"Your half-sister?" Clearly astonished, Euan nonetheless nodded grimly. "Whoever took Lisette must have been given your description, and with the two of you so favoring each other—och, I'll slay the man as soon as I catch him!"

He stormed from the room with Isabeau running after him down the hallway, followed by Sister Damaris. Yet he stopped just before reaching the door to the sleeping quarters and spun to face them.

"I'll post guards all around the convent. Once her captor discovers his mistake, he may try tae come back for you and they'll be waiting for him. I'd swear on my life that Robert the Bruce lies at the heart of this plot tae steal my intended bride on the eve of our wedding! Aye, an attempt at revenge for his traitorous brothers' execution, but our marriage this very hour will thwart him."

Isabeau gasped as Euan grabbed her by the hand and pulled her with him out the door as he barked an order at Sister Damaris.

"Summon a priest from the adjoining abbey, Reverend Mother, and tell him tae meet us in the chapel. Go!"

With a nod, the older woman went running, her black habit flapping around her legs. Isabeau hastened alongside Euan, doing her best to keep up with his long strides.

"We're to marry today?"

"Aye, not the grand occasion I envisioned for us," Euan said as they reached the convent chapel, Isabeau breathless now and half stumbling up the steps. "Nor the wedding night, but there's no help for it. I dinna know how long it will take me tae find your half-sister, so I must leave as soon as the ceremony is done."

A quick look around told Isabeau that they were alone as Euan drew her into an alcove and pressed her to the wall. She guessed his intent before he even yanked her silk tunic above her hips, and then hoisted up his own tunic and clutched her bare bottom to draw her against him.

"Consummation before the blessing, but we've no time tae spare, aye?" he said thickly, not waiting for an answer as he thrust his swollen flesh into her, Isabeau gasping at the sudden piercing pain.

All she could do was hold onto him and think of the jewels...*anything* for the jewels, her hatred for Lisette growing all the hotter as Euan rutted against her, his loud groans echoing from the chapel walls.

CHAPTER 4

"Shetill sleeps, Laird Campbell?"

Conall nodded at the balding middle-aged priest, as unsettled to hear himself called *laird* as that Isabeau had barely fluttered an eyelash since he and his men had stopped to rest for a few hours.

An owl hooted from a high branch, the trees so dense where they had taken shelter that he had deemed it safe enough to build a warming fire against the night's cool dampness. Sighing heavily, he drew the blanket up beneath Isabeau's chin, her lovely features illuminated by the flickering flames.

"If I might ask, how much potion did you give her? It doesna take much tae induce sleep—"

"*Too much*, Father Titus," Conall cut him off grimly, scowling. "Does that satisfy you? If she never wakes, it will be my fault alone. One more transgression tae send me straight tae hell."

"Och, Laird, no, you mustna say such things!" the priest countered, crossing himself. "I'm praying for the lass...and for you, that all will be well."

Conall felt a tic working along his jaw as he watched Father Titus hasten back to his blanket and lie down, following the lead of the fourteen men who were stretched out upon the ground, asleep.

Another six warriors guarded the perimeter of their camp, their shapes barely visible in the darkness, while Conall turned his attention back to Isabeau.

Och, the poor lass! What had he done to her?

He should never have made her swallow the entire vial, but everything had happened so fast. He'd had barely enough time to subdue her, wrap her in a cloak, and then carry her from the women's quarters—aye, with that old nun's scream ringing in his ears—as haste had been of utmost importance to the success of his mission. He couldn't help wondering again if that gullible young novice had suffered for allowing him entrance into the convent compound, but then he thrust the thought away.

He hoped not, but he could do nothing to help her... and there didn't appear to be anything he could do to help Isabeau, either.

She slept so soundly, too soundly. Anyone might have thought her dead if not for the gentle rise and fall of her breasts.

Aye, her form covered up by the blanket and the cloak that still enshrouded her, but there was no mistaking the curved outline of her body that made Conall's loins grow tight.

By God, was he a barbarian to lust after an unconscious woman? His future bride, aye, but he had no idea if she would ever wake from the brew that had left her limp in his arms the entire ride to this secluded spot. He had told her that he wouldn't hurt her, but what was she now? He would rather she was glaring at him and cursing him for abducting her than in this endless sleep—

"No...no...not my necklace..."

Conall felt his breath catch at the soft sound of her voice, the first time he had heard her speak. Sitting beside her, he edged closer so he might hear if she murmured anything else, but she only tossed her head from side to side and then once more grew still.

Och, but at least it was some movement! Some sign that she might be coming out of the stupor that had enveloped her for hours.

Conall saw that Father Titus had heard her words, too, for he had lifted his head to glance in their direction—though he lay back down and tightly folded his hands once again in prayer.

The man's lips moved, but no sound came, which made Conall send his own silent appeal heavenward that the lass would be fully recovered by morning.

What necklace had she spoken of? He did not recall that she'd worn any jewelry when he first saw her. A gift from MacCulloch?

Shrugging away that thought, Conall could not resist reaching out to touch a dark lock of hair that glistened with red in the firelight—och, so soft, like the feel of her cheek when he had wiped away a tear that morning.

Isabeau *was* beauteous, just as King Robert had told him, though Conall felt certain that her lovely features would contort with hatred once she opened her eyes again.

Aye, once she realized that she was far away from Dumfries and her betrothed and was soon to marry another man against her will. Conall had every expectation that she would kick and scream and fight him every step toward the altar of the village church that lay several hours' ride from where they had camped tonight.

Her outraged cries of protest ringing from the rafters, though thankfully, they would be in territory loyal to King Robert, and not England.

"Ah, lass...it's not what I wish, either," Conall said under his breath, gently twisting a silken tendril around his forefinger. "Our lives are not our own, our paths decreed by others. I dinna want a bride and you dinna want *me*. A Highland warrior that never dreamed he would be the laird of anything, but now with a castle and lands awaiting him once I take you tae wife. Mayhap it would be better if you never awake for the unhappiness our marriage will bring you, Isabeau Charpentier—och, it's in God's hands."

With a heavy sigh, Conall let the curl slip from his finger and lay down beside her, pulling his own blanket up to his waist.

He needed sleep, too, for whatever the morrow might bring.

He had no doubt that Euan MacCulloch and his English-loving compatriots were searching high and low for her, but Conall and his men had ridden so hard and so fast after they reunited that no one would catch them now.

Another two days and they would reach Dumbarton Castle, but there was a lot to accomplish before that happened.

A wedding and a bedding—och, if the lass lived.

Conall glanced to the side and saw again in the gleam of firelight that her chest still rose and fell—but with a slight catch that made him look at her face.

No, she slept on...her features in gentle repose, which made him certain that he had imagined the unexpected movement.

Weariness overwhelming him, Conall rolled onto his side with his back to her and closed his eyes, the sputter and crackle of the flames lulling him to sleep.

~

Lisette blinked open her eyes the moment the huge Scotsman rolled away from her, though she didn't move an inch.

Her heart thundering, she glanced to her right at

the men sleeping around the fire—and then to the massive shoulders of the man lying to her left, his broad back blocking out any view on that side.

Dear God, he was the same man who had forced that foul-tasting liquid into her mouth, nearly causing her to choke. She could see that he wasn't dressed any longer in the habit of a friar, but in a dark tunic with a padded leather overshirt that she guessed must be some sort of armor. He had said he was a warrior, hadn't he? A Highland warrior...

Lisette sharply drew in her breath, her heart beating so fast now that she thought it might leap from her breast.

He had called her Isabeau Charpentier, too. *Isabeau*! That alone made the cobwebs still lingering in her mind disappear altogether, the astonishing reality of what must have happened hitting her with full force.

The man had abducted *her*, thinking she was her half-sister!

And he intended to take her to wife...but she was Lisette! What would this giant of a Scots Highlander do with her when he realized the truth?

Lisette squeezed her eyes shut and swallowed hard against tears threatening to spill, her mind racing.

A nightmare had drawn her out of the blackness...a terrible, recurring nightmare that had plagued her since Claudia had torn the necklace her father had given her from her neck and flung it into the fire.

That, and the sensation of someone touching her hair.

It had been all Lisette could do to lie still and breathe calmly, when she had wanted to scream in fear. Her first conscious thoughts a wild scramble of wondering where she was and what had happened to her.

Then she had heard a low husky voice speaking to her...a man's voice that she recognized at once.

The same man who had vowed he wouldn't hurt her

right after he had tilted that vial into her mouth, and said she would soon fall fast asleep—*mon Dieu*, he had given her a sleeping potion! The last thing she remembered was her limbs growing weak and the sensation of someone sweeping her off her feet. The friar, except he wasn't a man of God at all, but a warrior...

Now the tears did spill, but Lisette did not dare to wipe them away.

What else had he said? Ah, yes, something about his path being decreed by others and that he didn't want a bride. Why, then, would he have agreed to abduct a woman betrothed to another man? Yet he hadn't abducted Isabeau at all, but *her*! The circular spinning of Lisette's thoughts made her head pound as despair threatened to overwhelm her.

He had said, too, that a castle and lands awaited him...so that alone could explain why he had put his life in great peril for such a mission. No one but a powerful lord could bestow such a rich reward, mayhap even a king. If her captor realized she wasn't Isabeau, would he ride back with her to the convent to try again? Or would he simply dump her in these woods to fend for herself and return from whence he'd come, his mission foiled?

Lisette started at the hoot of an owl overhead, but it didn't seem to stir the man sleeping next to her. Some of the others were snoring and sputtering, but her captor didn't make a sound. She stared up at the dense branches aglow in golden firelight, her despair reaching such a crescendo that it felt like a knife cutting through her.

She didn't want to go back to Dumfries! Nor did she wish to see Isabeau ever again.

Her half-sister had made her life a misery since she could remember, and had threatened to marry her off to one of Euan MacCulloch's brutish warriors. Either way, a wedding lay in her future—but with this man, she might have a chance at a new life.

He must have been given some description of Isabeau to have mistaken Lisette for her, so why not pretend that she *was* her half-sister? They looked so much alike after all. God help her, if there was any mercy in heaven, it might work...

Lisette could have wept aloud for the hope that filled her, sweeping away her desolation as if it had never assailed her.

Yet what would Isabeau have done if she had found herself in Lisette's place? A young woman abducted from her betrothed? Surely not lie there like a lamb to the slaughter.

Isabeau would try to escape at her first opportunity, which made Lisette slowly lift her hands out from underneath the blanket, her heart once again racing.

If her captor was to believe she was Isabeau, she must try to escape, too, but which way?

Lisette glanced all around her, the thick, towering trees cloaked in shadow and appearing almost menacing. She heard a stick snap, which made her gasp and then bite her tongue.

She didn't relish the thought of running headlong into the dark forest with dangerous animals lurking—wolves and wild boar. Yet what choice did she have if she was to appear convincing as an abducted bride?

Gathering her courage, Lisette threw aside the blanket and jumped to her feet, though sudden dizziness nearly felled her.

She staggered a step, dragged down, too, by the heaviness of a cloak that had been wrapped snugly around her...oh, no, the burgundy cloak that had been made especially for Isabeau's wedding day. Lisette was certain her half-sister didn't care anything about her disappearance, but the loss of the beautiful gown and cloak must have infuriated Isabeau—

"Laird Campbell, the lady is awake! *She's awake!*"

Lisette stifled a scream at what appeared to be a priest jumping up from his blanket, which made her stumble forward to the nearest trees while the camp exploded into commotion all around her. Yet she had taken no more than another step when she was swept up into powerful arms, coming face-to-face with one of the most handsome men she had ever seen in her life.

She gasped as his hold upon her tightened, his deep voice ringing out around them.

"Steady, men, I've got her. Go back tae your rest."

She gaped at him, not sure if his eyes were dark blue or black in the firelight, as he seemed to give her a fierce hug before striding back to where they had been lying.

"So you'll live after all, lass. You had me wondering for a while if I'd poisoned you with that healer's potion—"

"*Oui*, you could have killed me!" Lisette blurted, her outrage as genuine as anything Isabeau could have uttered. "Let me down, I've two good legs and can walk on my own—"

"Like you did a moment ago, staggering like a drunkard? You might have hurt yourself, Isabeau. Bumped your head against a tree trunk or twisted an ankle. What will I tell King Robert if any harm comes tae my bride? He sent me tae fetch you and I'd like you tae meet him safe and whole. Now lie down, woman, and go back tae sleep."

King Robert? Her mind spun as her strapping captor set her down upon the blanket with surprising gentleness, Lisette realizing that her abduction had been ordered by the highest authority, just as she'd guessed.

No, Isabeau's abduction, Euan MacCulloch one of young King Edward's most loyal Scots nobles, which made him one of King Robert's most hated enemies.

Suddenly Lisette remembered Euan boasting not

long after she and Isabeau had disembarked from the ship that he had helped to capture two of King Robert's own brothers earlier in the year...everything starting to make sense. Those wretched men had been put to death in the most horrible fashion—

"Have a sip of water, you look pale."

The man that the priest had called Laird Campbell bent down on one knee to offer her a drink from what appeared a wineskin, but Lisette turned her head just as she imagined Isabeau would have done. In truth, she felt thirsty and hungry, her stomach growling so loudly that her captor flashed a grin that made Lisette's breath catch.

"Och, lass, dinna fight me. I told you before that I wouldna hurt you."

"You already have," she countered, trying not to stare at him even as she thought again that she had never seen a man so handsome to look upon. "Mayhap you've slipped some potion in that water as well, just to tame me."

"Tame you?"

The huskiness in his voice gave her shivers, but it was the knowing way he looked at her that made her heart skip a beat.

"Ah, lass, you willna struggle when the time comes. You might as well know that you're tae become my bride tomorrow morning, so you can fight your fate or accept it—just as I've done. I'm Conall Campbell, and soon tae be your husband. Now take a wee draught or sleep the rest of the night parched as a stone, it's up tae you."

Tomorrow morning? Her thoughts spinning so wildly that Lisette could only nod, her fingers trembled as she held onto the wineskin he brought to her lips.

Conall nodded, too—*Conall*, such a fine strong name, she couldn't deny it—as if pleased that she drank, but then he drew away the wineskin.

"Not too much, Isabeau, it could make you queasy, so I'll not give you any food tonight, either. At dawn, you'll dine on oatcakes like the rest of us—aye, you see what I mean?"

Lisette had winced at the thought of eating anything, though her stomach pangs felt eased from drinking some water. He leaned forward to give her another sip, the masculine scent of him overwhelming her senses—sweat and horses and wood smoke, but it didn't repel her, no, not at all.

Conall seemed to inhale, too, though a quizzical look came upon his face that made her wonder what might be amiss. He shrugged his immense shoulders and stood up, outstretching his hand to her.

"Forgive me, it occurred tae me that you might need tae relieve yourself before you sleep."

"*Non*, I'm fine," she murmured, blushing to her roots, but he shook his head and reached down to pull her to her feet.

"A short walk will do you good, lass."

She didn't fight him, though from the raised heads of his men and the priest who had returned to their blankets on the ground, they seemed to anticipate a struggle. To her surprise, Conall gave a short laugh as if reading their thoughts and led her into the trees.

"Here, I'll take your cloak."

He whisked the garment from around her shoulders before she could answer. With the flames of the stoked fire lending some light to the surrounding forest, he gestured for her to venture a little deeper—she imagined, to grant her some privacy.

Lisette flushed again, though it was only a natural thing he bade her to do. She had no slippers, either, her feet bare, so mayhap that was why he believed she wouldn't try to thwart him.

She stepped around a thick tree trunk and then another, and lifted Isabeau's wedding gown so she could crouch down and quickly accomplish the task—which made her think again of what her half-sister would have done.

Yes, she was acting altogether too docile and pliant for the dreadful outrage that Isabeau would have believed was inflicted upon her. Lisette had no sooner stood up and dropped the gown back into place when she darted deeper into the woods, though she heard a wild crashing not far behind her.

"By God, woman, *stop!*"

CHAPTER 5

Lisette did not stop, her heart thundering as she plunged further ahead, nearly slipping on the damp earth. She knew Conall was close behind her from the sound of his heavy footfalls, which made her gasp for breath and dodge her way faster through the trees.

"Isabeau, dinna you hear the howling?" came his frustrated shout, which made her slow her step to glance to her right and left as fear gripped her.

Ah, God, *wolves*? She spun around at the same moment Conall careened into her, a scream bursting from her throat, though he caught her before she tumbled to the ground.

His breathing hard. His curse low and angry. His arms locking around her to pull her against him.

"Woman, dinna ever do that again. *Do you understand me?*"

She stared up at him, bobbing her head though she doubted he could see her acquiescence in the darkness. Only a glimmer of light emanated from the distant camp, his men's shouts echoing through the woods as they searched for her, too.

She heard it then, a wild howling from not too far away that made goosebumps prickle her skin. She felt

Conall spread his feet as if bracing himself, still holding her with one arm while he drew his sword from his belt with the other.

His breathing had slowed, the raw tension in his body telling her that he was preparing for whatever might lunge at them out of the trees.

More howling came, closer still. A whole chorus, this time punctuated by guttural growls that made Conall press her against a tree and stand in front of her —Lisette knew, to shield her from the attack.

An attack that came so suddenly, dark hulking shapes rushing at them from three directions even as two of the fearsome creatures were cut down by Conall's slashing blade.

Lisette cried out when he grunted from the force of a third wolf launching itself at him.

A terrifying snarl became a shrill yelp and then a whimper as the wounded animal collapsed at his feet.

A chunking sound silenced even that whimper, Conall driving his sword into the beast at the same moment sputtering torches appeared through the trees.

Several of Conall's men rushed toward them and drove away the rest of the pack, the wolves with their glittering orange eyes disappearing as quickly and stealthily as they had come.

"Laird Campbell, did you find her?"

In the torchlight, Lisette held her breath as Conall nodded at his men and turned to face her, his bloodied hand still gripping his sword.

"Do you hear me, Isabeau? *Never again.*"

He looked so fierce, so grim, that she could but nod at him, horror gripping her that he must have been bitten.

Ah, no, she had seen one of her father's huntsmen with such an injury succumb to a terrible sickness that had left him writhing and foaming at the mouth!

She had never known such relief when Conall

sheathed his sword and wiped his hand against his tunic, the blood coming away with no bite marks underneath.

"Y-you're not wounded?" she stammered.

Her knees nearly buckled when Conall shook his head. He seemed disinclined to say another word to her as he grabbed her by the elbow and drew her along with him through the trees, his men lighting the way with their torches. He only paused once, to retrieve the cloak he must have dropped to the ground when Lisette had darted away from him, but he didn't wrap it around her.

He remained silent until they reached the camp, the rest of his men surrounding them while the priest stood to one side, his hands tightly clasped in prayer.

"As you can see, Lady Isabeau is safe," Conall said without a glance at Lisette, who dropped her gaze at the disapproving looks his men cast her. "We've a few hours more until dawn. Let's get some rest while we can —*if* we can."

His grip on her elbow tightened as if warning her once more against making another rash move, Lisette not daring to lift her eyes as he led her back to her blanket.

She could not have succeeded more in acting the desperate captive, but she vowed to herself then and there she would never do it again—just as Conall had admonished her.

If he hadn't caught up with her, she would have been killed by those wolves. *He* could have been injured, too, or worse, her stomach roiling at the danger he'd faced to protect her.

Protect her.

No one had ever done such a thing for her other than her father, who had done his best to shield her from Claudia and Isabeau's cruelty until the day he died. With a vengeance, the two had then descended like mythic harpies upon her—no, she wouldn't think of them anymore!

Tomorrow she would marry Conall Campbell and never look back...and she would do nothing again to try and thwart him.

She could be more herself from now on, and he would think nothing of it other than that the young woman he believed was Isabeau had been thoroughly chastised by her reckless attempt to escape—and was now contrite.

So contrite.

He gestured for her to lie down and she did, without a word.

She didn't even look at him as he covered her first with the cloak and then with the blanket, though she was grateful for his thoughtfulness. The night air was cool and she shivered, which made him lean down and tuck the blanket around her shoulders.

"That should keep you warm enough. Get some sleep."

Only then did she meet his eyes, Lisette astonished to see no anger in his gaze...though his handsome features were still grim in the firelight.

She could not help staring at him, her breath catching at his masculine beauty.

His hair as black as night and grazing his broad shoulders. Everything about him exuding strength and power, from the breadth of his chest to the muscular litheness of his body as he straightened to tower over her. Her gaze fell to his hand still smeared with blood, which made her stomach flip all over again.

"Are you sure you're not wounded, Laird Campbell? I would never forgive myself..."

Lisette had fallen silent at the startled look he gave her, his tone now not half so gruff.

"Aye, lass."

He didn't say anything more. With a sigh of weariness, he settled down onto his own blanket—though this time, he didn't roll over and turn his back to her.

Instead, Lisette felt him watching her as she closed her eyes to try and sleep.

Saints help her, how could she rest with him lying so close to her? Tomorrow night at this time, mayhap they wouldn't be lying upon blankets on the ground, but sharing a warm bed somewhere as man and wife.

Laird Conall Campbell, her husband!

Conall stared at Isabeau with some consternation, the sweetness of her last words not what he would have expected from her at all.

I would never forgive myself...

Aye, she'd said it, he had heard her, the poignant concern in her voice having soothed him more than he cared to admit.

He should still be pacing the camp in fury for her daring to run away from him!

He should have tied her to a tree so there would be no chance of another escape attempt, instead of allowing her to sleep unfettered on the blanket.

He could tell that she wasn't sleeping from the rapid pulse beating at the base of her throat...and a lovely throat, too.

Pale like alabaster, just as King Robert had said. Her beauty rare indeed, with her lustrous dark hair flecked with red against so fair a complexion, her delicate features in perfect proportion from her winged brows to her lush red lips.

God help him, how was he to sleep with so wondrously fashioned a woman lying next to him, no more than a forearm's reach away?

He could hear the rise and fall of her breathing, not at all the gentle repose as when she hadn't yet awakened from the potion, but faster and shallower as if she could not sleep, either. Was she thinking of trying to evade him again? Her kindhearted concern just another way to deceive him and lull him into thinking she had accepted her fate—when all the while she was plotting her next move?

Now Conall did roll onto his back, though he had no intention of sleeping.

He couldn't risk her slipping away again in a forest full of wolves—och, he didn't want to think of it! If he hadn't caught up with her in time...

Conall shoved the grisly thoughts away and glanced over to see that her breathing seemed to have slowed down a wee bit, a good sign. Either that, or she sensed him still watching her and wanted him to think she had truly settled down for the rest of the night—aye, but he didn't trust her any more than he wanted to take a bride.

He doubted he would ever be able to trust her—or her, him—for how they had started out in life, with an abduction. Odd, it occurred to him then that she hadn't asked him about what had happened at all, or the why of it, but mayhap she had surmised all she needed to know for now.

He had told her that King Robert had made him fetch her and that they would be wed in the morning. What else was there to say? Yet for a woman that had been torn from her betrothed, he would have expected more screams and tears.

The only outrage Isabeau had shown him was that the potion could have killed her. No demands at all about what lay at the heart of her abduction. Conall thought she would have wanted to know right away, but mayhap she was as clever as she was beautiful and had already surmised her former husband-to-be's support of King Edward had made her a tempting target.

Or mayhap Euan MacCulloch had boasted to her of

his part in capturing King Robert's two brothers—aye, and she had already guessed that revenge for their execution had fueled her sudden change of fate.

Bitterness swelled inside Conall that Isabeau might have been proud of MacCulloch's role in so heinous a crime, but let him not forget that she was from France. What did she truly know of the hatred between those Scots loyal to England and King Robert's supporters?

Och, she would learn soon enough after their marriage tomorrow. Conall had no intention of being heavy-handed with her, but he would forbid her from ever speaking of any loyalty to England, whether she harbored some herself or not!

Heaving a sigh, Conall rubbed his hands over his face, his body craving sleep no matter he should stay awake to watch over Isabeau.

The wolf had leapt upon him with tremendous force, the snarling creature's massive paws striking his chest. He felt bruised and sore, but there was no healer with a remedy until he returned to Dumbarton Castle. Regretting again throwing away the basket that had held liniment for such aches, Conall did his best to stay awake though his eyes kept drifting closed.

He knew the guards positioned around the camp would shout out to him if Isabeau tried to escape, but even the slightest chance that they might miss her and she run into the woods—

"Blast and damn!" Conall smiled wryly that he sounded so much like his elder brother Cameron, but those accursed wolves were no laughing matter. He rolled back onto his side and shifted closer to Isabeau, not caring that he was no longer lying upon the blanket.

As a warrior, he had slept many times in stinking mud mixed with blood from battle. What did a few hours upon the cold ground matter? Or the daggers that would soon fly at him from Isabeau's eyes when he drew her against him and tightened his arm around her?

At least he would know that she was safe. If she tried to flee again, he would awaken in a flash—

"Oh!"

It wasn't daggers that greeted him as he pulled her into his embrace, but wide-eyed surprise, Isabeau gaping at him.

To his surprise, she didn't struggle, though she did stiffen against him.

Not in protest, he sensed from the rapid rise and fall of her breasts beneath the weight of his arm, but mayhap from panic. Had she not been held by a man before? Had MacCulloch not once hugged her or kissed her since she had arrived in Dumfries?

A jolt of something akin to jealously coursed through Conall, and he thrust away the unsavory thought. He had felt such an emotion only once before, when his honey-haired Lorna had told him that she had chosen to marry a blacksmith over him. Conall had wanted to ride into the village that very hour to kill the man—

"Please...I-I can't breathe!"

Conall loosened his hold, which had tightened like a band of iron around Isabeau just to think of his former love's betrayal.

"Forgive me," he murmured, not knowing what else he could say as she stared up at him with the softest brown eyes he had ever seen. Not angry at all...but frightened.

Dear God, he didn't want to scare the lass or distress her any more than their marriage would in the morning. Would she weep tears for Euan MacCulloch? Scowling, Conall thrust away that thought, too, and eased his hold even further.

"Try tae rest," he whispered into her ear, the warmth of her skin so near that he longed suddenly to nuzzle her neck.

Strange, how this close to her, she bore not a whiff

47

of lilac when her bedchamber had been filled with the scent. He had noticed that earlier when giving her a drink of water, yet why wouldn't she smell now of fresh air and wood smoke from the fire? Somehow he refrained from drawing any closer, reminding himself of why he had edged over to her side.

"Mayhap we'll both get some sleep now since I'll know if you try tae run away."

"I won't run away, Laird Campbell, I promise. Thank you for saving my life."

So startled again that he could but stare at her, Conall told himself fiercely in the next moment that her soft words weren't heartfelt.

How could they be? No matter she had relaxed within his embrace, her breathing growing slow and measured, Isabeau must surely hate him, and was only biding her time...

CHAPTER 6

"God's blessing on you both, Laird and Lady Campbell."

Lisette looked up at Conall, but he was staring at Father Titus with the strangest look upon his face as if he couldn't quite believe the brief marriage ceremony was done.

The entire morning thus far had been a blur of rising well before dawn, Conall speaking little to her as he had walked her into the trees again—staying closer this time—and then pressing a stale oakcake into her hand right before lifting her onto his horse. Amid a thundering of hooves, they had ridden an hour to a village with a small church in its midst, Conall's men waiting for them outside as only he, Lisette, and the priest had dismounted.

The sun had just peeked above the horizon, so the church was dark inside but for a single candle lit upon the white-clothed altar. At once the resident priest, an old man with stooped shoulders, had shuffled into the sanctuary from a side room, clearly awakened by the commotion. Father Titus had quickly introduced himself and told him that he needed to perform a wedding, and the old priest had stepped aside to allow him to officiate.

It seemed Lisette had no more than blinked and Conall had taken her hand and led her to the altar, his fingers gripping hers tightly as if he'd thought she might try to bolt—while Lisette had never felt such hopeful anticipation. With the candle sputtering and the musty air tinged with incense, she and Conall had uttered their vows…and now it was done.

Lisette had become Lady Campbell, her fingers trembling with relief as tears filled her eyes.

She was free of her half-sister forever!

"If you're crying for Euan MacCulloch, lass, I dinna want tae hear of it—ever. He's dead tae you now, do you hear me?"

Lisette bobbed her head at Conall's terse words, an expression on his face that she couldn't read though she sensed he wasn't pleased from his darkened eyes.

Not black at all, but the deepest blue in the candle-light. Still gripping her hand, he turned abruptly from the altar and led her down the narrow aisle to the church door.

"I knew this wedding would bring you unhappiness, but now you're my bride—though God knows, I swore never tae wed."

He spoke the last words with so much bitterness that Lisette wondered why he would have ever made such a vow, but Father Titus calling out to them made Conall whirl around.

"*What*, man?"

"You've forgotten about the church record, Laird."

Lisette felt her heart jump, though she hastened alongside Conall to one side of the church where the old priest awaited them by a small table.

What was she going to do? If the record bore only Isabeau's name, would that invalidate the marriage?

"Conall Adair Campbell," he said to the priest, who dipped a pen with shaky fingers into a small bowl of ink and scratched the name onto the parchment.

When he was done, the old man settled his watery gaze upon Lisette, Conall squeezing her hand.

"Go on, lass. Mayhap not the name you wanted, but yours now, all the same."

She nodded, swallowing hard against her sudden nervousness, her voice coming out in a strained squeak. "Lisette Isabeau Charpentier—f-forgive me, Campbell."

"*Lisette?*"

Conall looked so sharply at her that she almost faltered.

"*Oui*...but my family called me Isabeau. My mother thought it a prettier name."

"Mayhap, though if Lisette is your true given name, which one do you prefer?"

She gaped at Conall, the thoughtfulness of his query startling her after he had been so somber since entering the church. Somehow she stammered, "L-Lisette."

"Aye, well, you could have told me already so I hadna been calling you by the wrong name. Lisette suits you better, if the truth be told."

If the truth be told? Lisette felt her cheeks flare hot to have lied so boldly in a house of God, but what else could she have done? As Father Titus drew closer to inspect the church record, the old priest finally finished with his laborious scrawling, she looked down at the floor only to gasp when Conall once again drew her along with him.

"The wedding is done. Now on tae the other. We've a full day's ride ahead of us, and then we'll spend the night in Lanarkshire with an ally of King Robert."

Lisette gulped, her face flushing even hotter, though Conall didn't seem to notice as he shoved open the door, the bright sunlight nearly blinding her.

They had entered the church only a short while ago with dawn breaking, the wispy clouds streaked with pink and orange and gold—but now it seemed as if the world had come alive all around them.

Birds chirping. Honeybees buzzing by. Cows mooing and goats bleating. Villagers going about their morning chores as if the armed warriors clustered outside the church didn't alarm them at all.

She realized then, as a breeze tinged with the sweet scent of wildflowers lifted her hair, that they must have arrived at a place loyal to King Robert. Why else would Conall have stopped at this particular church? She felt so giddy all of a sudden for the new life bestowed upon her by heaven that Lisette couldn't help smiling, a laugh breaking from her throat.

At once Conall stopped in his tracks to stare at her, a look of bewilderment on his face.

"Something amuses you?"

For an instant she didn't know what to say, imagining what he must be thinking...that she hadn't just acted at all like a young woman abducted and made to marry a stranger—but nor had she since he'd awoken her. She hadn't fought him or screamed or burst into tears, well, other than the ones he had misread at the end of the ceremony.

Yet let him think what he would! She had never felt so happy. She beamed such a smile upon him that she saw a flicker of a smile light his face, too, no matter Lisette sensed he had done so in spite of himself.

"A beautiful day, isn't it?"

He nodded, though he sobered, looking at her now with outright suspicion.

"Do you feel well, wife? Mayhap the effects of the potion still linger..."

Wife. Lisette felt so lighthearted in that moment, so thankful for having been released from the wretched prison that had once been her life, she couldn't help laughing again.

"Aye, the potion, it must be," she heard Conall mutter as he took her by the arm and led her to his horse, the massive animal snorting and tossing its head.

Nothing could dampen her mood, no, not even her new husband's scowl as he lifted her into the saddle and then hoisted himself up behind her to hold her close.

Poor Father Titus barely made it onto his own steed before Conall gave a shouted command for his men to set off.

Lisette leaned her head against his shoulder as his strong arms tightened around her, and she even went so far as to wave gaily at the old priest, who waved back at her, while Conall's incredulous curse rang in her ear.

"Do you know the caliber of the man you've married, lass? Mayhap Conall isna as famed as his former commander, Gabriel MacLachlan, or his older brother Cameron, but he's as fearsome as they come on the battlefield. I've seen it myself from fighting alongside him! A toast tae you and your bride, Campbell!"

Conall raised his ale cup along with James Douglas, a dark-haired giant of a man who tossed down the foamy brew with one long swallow and then slammed the empty vessel upon the table.

"More ale for my honored guests and be quick about it!"

At once servants scurried to obey him, Laird Douglas's booming command echoing from the rafters of the great hall as he leaned closer to Conall and lowered his voice.

"Didna you say your new wife understood our language? She hasna uttered a peep since we sat down at the table—och, man, look at her! I've rarely seen such an appetite in a lass, have you?"

Conall shook his head, feeling guilty that he hadn't had more to offer Lisette than days' old oakcakes since they had left the church that morning.

Sitting across from him with her hair tousled and

her gown mussed from their long ride, she dug into a second bowl of venison stew, her mouth full to bursting as a platter of roast pig was offered to her. She came close to tumbling from her chair in her eagerness to skewer a slice with her table knife, while James slapped Conall on the back and roared with mirth.

"Aye, she'll bear you sons for certain with that appetite! My wife was the same, God rest her. Have you ever seen such fine strapping lads as *my* sons? Stand up, the lot of you, so Laird Campbell can take a good look at you."

Chairs grated upon the stone floor as four young men at the end of the table stood up and bowed their heads in deference to Conall, which he had never experienced before. Yet he supposed he must become accustomed to such acknowledgement now that he would soon have a castle and lands of his own.

"My eldest, Roger, just turned twenty and my heir —aye, and chomping at the bit tae become laird of Douglas Castle if I ever fall in battle," James said in what Conall sensed was part jest, part stark reality. "Next tae him, William, barely a year between them. I'll not part with either of the lads for if Roger doesna outlast me, then his younger brother will become the laird."

Conall saw a look pass between Roger and William —both of them dark-haired and strapping like their father—that evidenced a simmering rivalry, but such was the way of the world.

As the youngest two of nine brothers, he and Cameron had no reason for jealousy and had always been close, their stern father having cast them out of the house as youths to make their way as hired warriors. Who would have imagined life would change so abruptly for them just from saving King Robert's life? James must have guessed his thoughts, for once again he leaned closer to Conall.

"Aye, you and Cameron have done well for your-selves—barons now, the two of you."

"*Baron?*" Conall echoed with surprise, noting that Lisette was close to finishing her stew, and mopped up the last wee bit of gravy with a crusty slice of bread. Something told him that she was listening to every word, though she focused intently upon her supper. "The king said nothing of that tae me—"

"Mayhap, but his message that you and your bride would stop here on your way north said as much—another well-deserved reward for securing his revenge against Euan MacCulloch, the fiend! Does the lass know that her once intended husband helped tae bring two of King Robert's brothers, Thomas and Alexander, tae their doom? The poor wretches hung by the neck and then drawn and quartered, their severed heads stuck high up on pikes for all tae see?"

If James Douglas's voice had been filled with good humor before, now he was glaring at Lisette as if daring her to answer. Conall saw her gulp and hastily swallow her food, her face flushing so bright red that he feared she might choke. A sudden rush of protectiveness over-came him, and he spoke up for her before Lisette could utter a word.

"Aye, how could she not know? She was tae marry the man, after all, but she's my wife now and all of that is behind her. Aye, Lisette?"

She bobbed her head and shoved away her bowl, her appetite clearly having fled. One of James's sons coughed as if to dispel the tension, a somber-looking young man with a crucifix hanging from a gold chain around his neck.

"A moment of prayer for the king's brothers, Father?" he queried, which made James sink back against his chair and throw a look of apology at Conall.

"Forgive me, Campbell, and your lovely lady, too. It's not her fault, just as you said—though I wish you'd cut

MacCulloch's throat as well as steal his bride. That's my third son, Evander, who wishes tae become a priest. Say your prayers later in the chapel, lad, we've dampened the mood enough for our guests as it is—"

"*I* will cut his throat one day, Father, if King Robert will grant me the task!"

Conall glanced at the fourth son who looked no more than fifteen, but already stood head to head with his elder brothers. His brown hair lighter and his eyes a steely gray, the lad brandished a gleaming knife he had pulled from his belt as James threw a look of great fondness at him.

"My youngest, David. Aye, and mayhap the fiercest of spirit, too. I'm thinking of sending him north tae Campbell Castle tae train as a warrior with your brother's men. Would Cameron have him?"

Conall nodded, though before he could speak, James rushed on.

"David's a fine boy, but impetuous and strong-willed and far too eager tae fight, as you can see. There's more tae being a warrior than wielding a sword, aye, Conall? At least if you want tae live long enough tae marry and sire a bairn or two—or more. By God, the hour is growing late! Go on, man, you and your new bride. If it was my wedding night all over again, I would have taken the lass tae bed already."

Conall heard Lisette's small gasp, but she didn't lift her eyes even when he arose and held out his hand to her.

For all the gaiety she had shown earlier in the day, perplexing him even now at what might have lain at the heart of it, now she appeared as nervous as any bride at what lay ahead. He could see that she trembled, which made him walk around the table and help her up from her chair.

What could he say that wouldn't fluster her further in front of James, his sons, their servants, and all the warriors, his own men and those of Clan Douglas, present in the hall?

"Come."

A simple command, and only then did she glance at him with fresh tears shining in her eyes, which made him sigh heavily.

So that was going to be the way of it. Yet the tremulous smile that lit her face did not match at all what he thought she must be feeling—God help him! What manner of young woman had he wed? Might it be possible that she hadn't wanted the marriage to MacCulloch after all and actually was glad that Conall had abducted her?

That thought made him grasp her hand and lead Lisette from the hall as James raised his cup in a ribald toast that their lovemaking break the bed beneath them, causing her to gasp again.

She seemed to have slowed her pace, which made Conall sweep her into his arms and carry her toward the tower where a chamber was prepared for them—cheers and whistles following them up the steps.

CHAPTER 7

"You've nothing tae fear, lass. I willna hurt you, but this is the way of things between a man and wife. You understand what we must do, aye?"

Standing in the middle of the well-appointed bed-chamber where Conall had set her down, Lisette met his gaze and nodded, though her chin trembled.

In truth, she felt no fear, though she was certain her pounding heart might leap from her breast. Since their wedding that morning, she had thought of little else than the bedding that must occur, for without a con-summation, she would not fully be a wife.

And she needed to be fully a wife! The final step in the miracle that had freed her from Isabeau and would bind her more deeply to Conall Campbell.

Her husband.

Lisette could but stare at him, standing there so tall and handsome in the golden light from a half dozen ta-pers lit around the room, which had been made as com-fortable for them as possible.

A warming fire in the fireplace heaped with crack-ling logs.

A bed more than large enough for two and sprinkled with sprigs of heather that scented the air.

A table set with two goblets and a decanter of what she imagined must be wine.

A white linen nightgown draped over a chair next to Lisette's cloak, which servants must have brought up to the bedchamber along with a leather bag containing Conall's belongings.

All this she had noted upon first glance when he had carried her into the room, but what made her cheeks burn now as she glanced beyond him was the large metal tub placed near the fireplace.

Empty, though a rap upon the door made Lisette gasp in surprise and Conall to wheel around as a small army of servants entered and began to carry in buckets of steaming water.

It seemed in no more than a few moments the task was done, the door shut, and she and Conall once again looking at each other as the servants' footfalls faded down the hall.

No other sound but that of their breathing...and the sputtering fire.

"Go on, Lisette...while the water is warm. I'll wash up in the basin."

He had spoken so low, his voice huskier than she had heard it before, which made shivers tumble to her toes as she nodded.

Yet she couldn't seem to move, feeling rooted to the floor while Conall left her to fetch the basin from a table set against the wall and then dip it into the tub to fill it.

Before she knew it, he had returned the basin to the table and methodically began to strip...first his sword belt, then his leather armor, and finally his tunic, which he pulled over his head.

Lisette stared in wonder as the most beautiful man she had ever seen glanced over his shoulder at her, his black hair tousled, his naked body rippling with muscle —and inclined his head toward the tub.

"You'd best undress before the water grows cool. Do you need help with your gown?"

As if his query had released her from a spell, Lisette shook her head and hastened over to the tub.

Her heartbeat racing.

Her hands shaking as she glanced behind her to see that Conall was focused upon his task of squeezing the water from a wadded cloth and running it over his body —which made her gulp and turn back to the fire.

She felt so flustered that she scarcely realized she had pulled the silken gown over her head and tossed it to the floor until she climbed into the tub and sat down, a sigh escaping her at the wondrous warmth of the water.

She had rarely known such a luxury in her father's home, thanks to Claudia and Isabeau, but Lisette shoved away the unhappy thoughts of ice-cold baths and reached for a square of soap at her feet—another luxury made soft and pliant in the water. She could not help sighing again as she ran the soap along one arm and then the other, the sweet fragrance of lavender wafting to her.

"Do you like that scent?"

Lisette gasped and twisted around to see that Conall watched her from where he toweled himself dry, his deep blue eyes darkened in the firelight. She spun back around in a spray of water and sank further into the tub, her knees raised.

"*Oui*, lavender is my favorite," she said in a breathless whisper, overcome again by his masculine beauty as she heard his footfalls cross the floor.

Not toward the bed to await her there...but to the tub.

Lisette lost her grip on the slippery soap that dropped with a plunk into the water, when she realized Conall had stopped just behind her.

"Hmm...I would have thought it lilac."

Lisette froze as Conall moved to the side of the tub and sank to his knees, a towel draped around his neck and covering his upper chest, his thickly muscled arm reaching into the water to retrieve the soap.

Lilac. Isabeau's favorite scent, *not* hers.

Lisette remembered then that her half-sister had doused herself in the fragrance before she had dressed, the smell trailing after Isabeau when she had hastened from the room. Of course Conall would think Lisette loved the scent, when in truth, she would forever associate it with her half-sister's cruelty...

"Euan gave me a vial of lilac perfume as a gift," Lisette said shakily, concocting a lie even as she wondered if Conall had thought it strange that she hadn't reeked of the scent. "It's his favorite—"

"Then I'll ask you tae never wear it again. Will that grieve you?"

She shook her head so quickly that he seemed surprised, and then a look of understanding lit his handsome features.

"Did you love the man you were tae wed?"

Lisette gaped at him, so stunned that Conall would ask her such a question that she didn't know quite what to say other than the utter truth. "No."

To her surprise, he looked almost relieved, though his expression then seemed to darken.

"Were you forced into the betrothal?"

Lisette shook her head again. She didn't want to fabricate any more lies, but there was nothing else she could do than offer Conall half-truths. "The marriage was arranged by my father some months before he died, at the behest of King Edward. An alliance between great families to draw England and France closer together—"

"Great families? I know nothing of the Charpentiers, but the *MacCullochs*?"

Conall had fairly spat the name, a scowl on his face

now that was frightening to behold. Lisette thought of enemies he must have faced in battle with such a forbidding countenance and she shivered, her skin prickling with gooseflesh.

"I can well understand why you would hate them," she murmured, feeling suddenly sick at heart at her realization, "but I had no part in the death of King Robert's brothers. Will you hate me, too, no matter we're now husband and wife?"

As if her query had doused him with cold water, Conall didn't look fearsome any longer as much as perplexed. He gave a short laugh, though Lisette could tell it held no humor.

"I dinna hate you, lass, but I'm not pleased by our marriage, I canna lie tae you. I didna wish tae marry *anyone*...and yet here we are."

The same bitterness in his tone that she'd heard after their wedding, Lisette almost blurted then and there that she wasn't Isabeau...as if that might make some difference to him. She wasn't an enemy, just a bastard daughter of no consequence at all and so grateful to him for freeing her—

"You're a strange one, Lisette Isabeau Campbell. I'd swear you were made glad by our wedding, though I canna fathom why."

Lisette blinked at Conall, deciding it was best to hold her tongue though she wondered wildly what he would think if he knew he had just hit upon the truth.

"Tae have your life upturned and yet you havna fought me. You havna screamed or kicked or tried tae strike me—aye, just run into the woods. Thank God I caught up with you in time."

At his reference to the wolves, Lisette shivered again, though she wasn't sure if it was more because Conall had flung aside the towel and begun to rub the soap between his large, calloused hands.

"You should be the one filled with hatred, wife, but I dinna see a trace of it in you—"

"I don't hate you!"

Her outcry silencing him, Lisette stared at Conall as he stared back at her, his eyes appearing darker in the firelight.

Dark as night and filled with something she couldn't fathom, either, the intensity making her drop her gaze to his chest.

Only then did she notice the two purple bruises in the shape of paw prints where the snarling wolf must have struck him—*massive* paw prints. Without thinking, she reached out to touch his chest with shaking fingers, terrible remorse filling her.

"I'm so sorry, Conall...so sorry."

Springy black hair beneath her fingertips, Lisette felt the beating of his heart, too, which had seemed to jump at her touch. She sucked in her breath and pulled back her hand, but he caught it with hard fingers slippery with soap.

"Lie back now and be still," he murmured thickly, Lisette obliging him with no thought of struggling as he used his other lathered hand to caress her shoulders and then slip down over her breasts.

She gasped at the sensation, his darkened gaze holding hers as his palm rubbed lightly across her nipples, swollen now into nubs that tingled at his touch.

Yet she jerked when his hand slid down her trembling abdomen to between her raised knees, dipping into a place that tingled, too, as his fingers caressed her.

"Does that please you, lass?"

He had spoken barely above a husky whisper, while all Lisette could do was nod for the sigh escaping her throat. His fingers circling and circling, his thumb flicking at another swollen nub she knew lay at the heart of her thighs...for she had touched herself there before, though she had been hesitant and unsure.

She jerked again and moaned, trembling now from head to toe as Conall caressed her, the circling pressure of his fingers anything but unsure. Still he held her gaze and she could not look away, moaning and open-mouthed at the sensations she'd never before felt building inside her.

She could no longer lie still no matter what he had bade her, her legs shaking, her hips pressing as if with a mind of their own against the weight of his teasing fingers—ah, God!

Lisette stiffened and threw back her head, crying out at the climax rocking her, water sloshing out upon the floor...while a slow smile spread over Conall's face that made her think he must be pleased as well by her response.

Somewhere in the back of her dazed mind, as she caught her breath, his hand straying up again to a hardened nipple, she was certain that he must be practiced at lovemaking to have brought her so deftly to such a state. Meanwhile she knew nothing—*nothing!*—of how to give pleasure to the man who was now her husband—

"The water is growing cool, Lisette. Stand up so I can rub you dry."

She gasped at his low command, not sure at all if she could rise up on legs still trembling while he only laughed and hoisted her from the tub.

Dripping wet with her long hair plastered to her body, she stood before him while he gazed upon her in so hungry a manner, she shivered anew.

"You're so beautiful, lass...so beautiful."

It seemed he had forgotten all about toweling her dry, for in the next moment he picked her up into his arms and strode with her to the bed.

The next thing Lisette knew, she was lying there with him on all fours above her, his hands splayed on each side of her head and his knees pressing against her hips.

His eyes burning into hers and appearing black now, Conall so big and muscular that all else around her was blocked out but for him.

His breathing growing harder as his powerful arms seemed taut with tension. The masculine smell of him melded with the woodsy scent of heather filling her senses and making her breathe faster, too.

"I said I wouldna hurt you...but some pain will come with the bedding, Lisette, forgive me."

She had barely nodded when he blanketed himself upon her and prodded her legs open with his knee, though it was his fingers again that made Lisette spread herself wider for him.

Teasing fingers slicked by the warm wetness of her body that made her squirm beneath his weight, her lips pressed to his ear.

"Oh, Conall...*Conall*!"

His name ringing around them, she made to scream at the piercing pain of him thrusting into her, but no sound came for his mouth covering hers.

His kiss fierce and possessive, his ragged breathing melding with her panting moans.

The pain was gone, something far more intense in its place, Lisette throwing her arms around his neck to hold him close.

To hold him tightly as he moved inside her, so deep that she knew little else but the weight of him upon her and the sensations building with his every thrust.

Still he kissed her, his tongue sweeping into her mouth at the trembling height of her release, Conall's body shuddering, too, as he groaned out her name against her lips.

A heart-stopping moment later and she felt herself drifting down, down, even as he collapsed on top of her, though not for long.

With another groan he rolled to one side and drew her against him, sheltering her within the crook of his arm.

No blanket needed for the warmth that seemed to envelop them, Lisette closing her eyes and curling her hands against his sweat-slicked chest.

The manly scent of him and the heat of his body lulling her into a sated sleep even as Conall pressed a kiss to the top of her head...his fingers entwining in her damp hair.

~

"God help me..."

Conall's voice no more than a whisper, he gazed down at the woman he had just claimed as his wife...not feeling at all like he would have imagined.

His lower body still throbbed for the seed that he'd spilled into her, his climax more intense than anything he had known since Lorna—

"No, you willna think of her!" he muttered even as he drew Lisette closer, her flushed cheek pressed to his chest, her soft, sweet breath fanning him.

Aye, soft and sweet, for so it seemed was everything about her...this woman that he had wed against his will. Their marriage decreed by a king, so how could Conall have refused?

He had done his part. Wedded and bedded her— och, how he had bedded her! He had not meant to take her so swiftly and fiercely, but his desire for her had overcome him, overtaken him.

In truth, he had never seen a woman fashioned so exquisitely as Lisette standing naked in front of him fresh from her bath.

Her creamy skin flushed pink from the steamy water.

Her wet body glistening with moisture in the glow of firelight like a golden sheen upon her.

Her breasts high and taunting, her swollen nipples framed by rosy aureoles that he ached to touch, even now.

With a groan, Conall felt himself growing hard again, so hard it hurt, but he would not wake her. The lass needed a good night's sleep after the rampant pace of the last two days.

Two days! That was all he had known her, and yet he was hard-pressed to imagine life without her...which made him groan.

He did not want to feel himself so drawn to this woman—nor to any woman! From the first moment he had seen her, she had not acted at all like he had imagined.

Aye, she had struggled at the convent...a bit.

She had tried to escape into the woods, but not so far that he hadn't been able to find her, as if she had made only a half-hearted attempt.

She had seemed joyous upon their wedding—aye, *joyous!*—which amazed him still. Her hearty appetite in the great hall not that of a woman mourning the loss of a life she had dreamed of—her marriage arranged or no.

The revelations she had made to him in so short a time just as astounding. Her words spoken with such sincerity and, with what he was certain, blunt honesty.

She didn't love Euan MacCulloch.

She didn't hate *him*, Conall Campbell.

Lisette showing such concern for him after he'd saved her from the wolves, and her soft, heartfelt apology when she had reached out to touch the bruises on his chest—

"Enough!" Conall whispered fiercely, but mayhap still too loud not to disturb Lisette's slumber when she stirred against him.

Her lovely hands curled into balls like a child's, she snuggled closer, which made him groan again.

He did not want to feel such emotion, such confusion, such bewilderment for any woman, least of all the bride that had been thrust upon him!

Cursing under his breath, Conall carefully disengaged himself from her so as not to wake her and rolled upon his back to stare at the ceiling.

Yet in the next instant when she sighed so sweetly in her sleep, he rolled back over, pulling the heather-sprinkled spread with him to cover them both.

Lisette once again nestled in his arms, her cheek pressed against his heart, which seemed to beat faster with her so near...God help him.

CHAPTER 8

"**M**y half-sister is wed?"

Isabeau had fairly screeched her query as she stared at Euan in disbelief, her husband sweaty and unkempt as he nodded wearily.

"Aye. My men and I couldna have been more than a few hours behind the bastard who took her, his trail steering us north, just as I suspected. Ten leagues from Dumfries, he joined up with at least twenty other riders and set a hard pace—too hard for us tae catch up, even with them stopping tae rest for a few hours. We had tae stop, too, for the horses, but once we set out again, we found where they'd camped, the fire pit still warm. We tracked them tae a village church where an old priest said a marriage had taken place no more than an hour past—"

"But to whom?" Still so incredulous that Isabeau found it difficult to croak out the words, she grabbed Euan's arm. "Did the priest give a name?"

"Something better, wife...written in the church record, but curious, too." With a heave of exhaustion, Euan sank into a chair. "Pity these nuns have no ale tae offer me, but water will do. Pour me a cupful, will you?"

Isabeau wanted to shriek again that Euan would make such a demand when she felt desperate to hear what else he might have to say, yet she quickly obliged him. She must have paced back and forth across this wretched convent room a thousand times while awaiting his return, so what was one more?

Her hands shaking with agitation, she filled a cup with cool water from a decanter placed on a table near the bed, and then hastened back to him.

"Here, drink."

Water sloshed onto Euan's hand when she thrust the cup at him, her brusqueness making him meet her eyes.

"It's for my mouth, not my fingers, Isabeau."

His gaze didn't leave her as he took a long draught and drained the cup, and then handed it back to her. Her impatience mounting, she thought he might ask her for another, but instead his expression hardened as he glanced out the narrow window.

"Aye, a vengeful plot tae steal you away and marry you off tae another. Yet Robert's man married the wrong woman…Conall Campbell's his name. I know of him and his brother Cameron, both seasoned warriors, and their commander, Gabriel MacLachlan—och, at least he was until some weeks past when Earl Seoras was slain—"

"What are you speaking of?" Isabeau interrupted him shrilly, nearly beside herself now. "I don't understand—oh!"

Euan had grabbed her and set her down so hard upon his knee that she was wholly taken by surprise. She gasped when his hand found her breast, his fingers rough as he kneaded her.

"Have I married a shrew for you tae speak tae me thusly?" he said in a low voice tinged with anger. "Dinna forget who is master here, Isabeau—and it isna you."

She nodded as he pulled her against him to nuzzle her neck, his gruff laughter surprising her even more.

"It seems your half-sister took your name as part of her own, which means her new husband must believe he has the right woman—by God, it's too rich! I would give anything tae see Campbell's face when he realizes his mistake. The church record bore the name Lisette Isabeau Charpentier. Is that her true Christian name?"

"*Non*," Isabeau murmured. "Lisette Mathilde Charpentier."

"So it's just as I thought, yet why would she have concocted such a ruse? Was she afraid for herself if Campbell knew the truth? That he might abandon her somewhere or cause her harm? Or mayhap she did so because she *wanted* tae wed her captor and has no wish tae return tae your side. Is that the way of it, Isabeau?"

She shook her head, but Euan's kneading at her breast only grew rougher, which made her wince.

"Och, woman, I'm your husband now with only your best interests at heart. There's no need tae carry on with any lies. It occurred tae me after we were well into the chase that I never saw you show Lisette one moment of affection from the time you came ashore. Mayhap you dinna love her at all—and there's another reason you set me after her. Now I ask you again. Is *that* the way of it, wife?"

Isabeau swallowed hard, his hand clasping her breast so tightly that tears of pain sprang to her eyes.

She had sensed upon first meeting Euan that he was a hard man from the scowl lines etched deep into his face—not handsome, but not unattractive, either, and his body strong and well-muscled. Yet now she knew for certain that he wasn't to be trifled with or lied to—*oui*, she had truly wed her match. She didn't feel defeated... only resigned that her mother's fervent wish for the jewels to remain a secret would be thwarted.

"If you must know, husband, I've hated Lisette all my life—for that's how long I've been made to suffer her presence. The kitchen maid who bore her stole my father's love from my mother...and cursed me with a half-sister who did the same to me by stealing my fa-

71

ther's affection. Nothing I did made his eyes shine with love as they always did for Lisette. *Nothing.*"

Euan's hand had fallen still at her breast, Isabeau so filled with bitterness that she felt choked by it. Yet somehow she went on, wondering if what she was about to reveal would make him forgive her for deceiving him.

"I could not care if she lives or dies...but something else was stolen when Conall Campbell took her away, believing she was me. Something very precious that must be regained."

Euan stared at her, his hazel eyes darkening to a deep green as he reached up and entwined his fingers tightly in her hair, making her scalp sting.

"So you did lie tae me."

"Mayhap I did not want you to think me spiteful and vicious to hate Lisette so—"

"Or else you did not wish me tae share in what must be regained, aye, wife?"

Isabeau didn't answer, only stared deep into his eyes and nodded, wondering if in the next moment he would strike her. To her astonishment, he loosened his grip upon her hair and leaned closer, his breath fanning her face.

"I demand truth from you, Isabeau, in all things. How else am I tae trust you as we make our way together? Now what did Conall Campbell take that belongs tae *us*?"

His emphasis on the last word made her want to cringe that she had lost any semblance of independence from him—at least for the time being.

"Jewels...sewed into the hem of a cloak that he wrapped her in. My mother sold land and bought them for me as a gift—"

"Ah, I understand now. As shrewd a woman as you, then? How much land?"

"A third of my inheritance."

Isabeau felt Euan stiffen, a scowl deepening the lines between his thick brows.

"No wonder you sent me right after her—and if I'd known, woman, I would have pressed on until I found them. Once I discovered they were wed, there didna seem tae be any point tae continuing the hunt. She was only a bastard, after all. Now they've surely arrived in Dumbarton where Campbell will crow of my humiliation and parade around his bride—until he learns the truth about her. Aye, I wish I could be there tae see it!"

Now Euan threw back his head and laughed so hard that tears squeezed from his eyes and rolled down his face, though he still held fast to Isabeau. She could but stare at him in confusion, until at last he coughed and cleared his throat to regain his composure.

"As I rode back into Dumfries, some of the men I left behind met me with word that a nest of traitorous spies had been discovered in town—though one escaped tae the north. Riding straight tae Robert the Bruce, I'd wager, with news of your foiled abduction and our hasty wedding at the convent chapel. Och, God, tae see that false king's face, too, when he discovers his plot failed!"

Laughter shook Euan again while Isabeau frowned and tried to rise from his knee. He caught her and thrust her back down, planting a noisy kiss upon her cheek.

"Dinna fret, wife, I know what you're thinking. What of the cloak and its hidden treasure? We'll have it back, I vow tae you, but a subtler method will be needed than an out-and-out attack. Robert is not the only one with spies and other sundry sorts paid tae do his bidding. Now pull up your gown, I've a great hunger for you."

Isabeau did as he bade her and straddled him, taking some comfort as Euan shoved his hand between them to wrench up his own tunic, that she would one day see the jewels again.

Her jewels.

No matter what he might think, she would not be sharing them with him.

She knew now even more fully than when he'd taken her against the wall in the chapel that her new husband was a brute and a tyrant and would make her life a misery for lying to him, she was certain of it. She would have to find some way to rid herself of him once the cloak was retrieved—

"By God, woman, does Lisette know the jewels were sewn into the cloak?" Euan demanded thickly as he clutched Isabeau's bottom, the thought clearly just occurring to him. He let out a deep groan of relief when she shook her head and leaned down to kiss him.

"It was a secret between only myself and my mother," she murmured against his lips, moistening them with her tongue. "Now *our* secret, husband. Take me..."

He did, entering her with such force that Isabeau gasped, clutching at him as the chair pitched beneath them. The wooden legs scraping upon the floor with his every thrust, his every ragged groan, while she felt hatred glowing hot within her.

For Lisette—*oui*, for Euan, too. Let him think her pliant and eager to please him while in her heart now, their marriage was doomed before it had scarcely begun.

∼

"Wait here for me while I let King Robert know we've arrived."

Lisette nodded at Conall, who left her in the antechamber and went out an opposite door into the great hall of Dumbarton Castle. She could hear the rumble of people enjoying their supper, and imagined the king was present among them and would soon return with Conall to meet her.

Ah, God, to meet her. Nervousness overwhelmed her, her hands trembling at the thought of encountering so renowned and royal a personage. Guilt riddled her, too, that she had deceived Conall and wed him, but what else could she have done?

Her remorse had only mounted since they had left Douglas Castle early that morning, Conall holding her closely against him the entire way to Dumbarton.

His every touch thrilling her.

His every glance calling forth heated memories of the night before when he had claimed her as his bride.

Even now, her heart fluttered to think of it...his attentiveness and caring while giving her pleasure unlike anything she had known.

Their bodies melded into one, their ragged breathing merged into one, and his kiss...*oh, Conall's kiss.*

Lisette pressed her fingers to her lips as a deep yearning overwhelmed her, for he hadn't kissed her since.

She had awakened at dawn to find him gone, a serving maid sent to help her dress in the only gown she possessed, soiled and rumpled from the last few days' journey, the burgundy cloak that had fared much better, and a pair of slippers scrounged up to shod her bare feet. Then she had been taken to him, Conall and his men already mounted on their horses and awaiting her in the bailey.

Laird Douglas and his sons gathered to bid them farewell. The youngest, David, had stepped forward to lift her into Conall's arms, the young man strapping and strong and smiling broadly to hear Conall assure him that he would speak to Cameron about David coming to train with his men.

Little had been said between her and Conall the entire day as they had ridden hard to reach Dumbarton

Castle before nightfall—and now they were here. To meet the king. Lisette gasped as the door leading from a hallway that she and Conall had come through moments ago suddenly opened, a sturdily built man entering that she guessed at once must be King Robert.

How could he not be from his powerful stride and air of authority that rippled through the air? His dark gray tunic a fine one and a tartan garment in hues of blue and green draped from his broad shoulder and wound around his waist, just like Conall had worn today instead of his leather armor, calling it a breacan.

The king stopped a few feet away from her, his large hands fisted at his waist as he looked her up and down in so forbidding a fashion that Lisette felt a chill. She glanced at the opposite door in desperate hope that Conall might return from the great hall, but King Robert clearing his throat made her gaze fly back to him.

His light brown eyes burning into hers, his fists clenched even more tightly, and his broad face made ruddy with anger.

"I dinna like being made the fool...and I doubt Conall Campbell, either. When I summon him tae join us, lass, will you tell him the truth about who you really are—or shall I?"

76

CHAPTER 9

Lisette gulped, a terrible realization hitting her that made her tremble to her toes.

Dear God, the king must know she wasn't Isabeau!

For an endless moment, she couldn't find any words to say, her tongue feeling wooden in her mouth—until with a ragged sigh, she sank to her knees in front of him and bowed her head.

"F-forgive me, my lord—*forgive me*!" Tears filling her eyes, she could not find the courage to look up at him even as he took a step toward her. "I'm Lisette Mathilde Charpentier—*non*, Lisette Campbell now since we were wed yesterday morning...and I will tell Conall the truth if you will allow it."

She fell silent, hot tears tumbling down her cheeks to fall upon the bodice of her gown—*Isabeau's* wedding gown. Yet no response came from the king as if he were waiting for her to continue, the displeasure emanating from him filling her with raw fear.

Would he throw her into a prison cell? Mayhap something worse?

"I-I know Conall meant to abduct my half-sister, but he mistook me for her and abducted me instead. I would have told him and I tried to fight him, but he forced a sleeping potion down my throat—"

"That is true."

Lisette gasped at the grim sound of Conall's voice, and glanced over her shoulder to see him standing just inside the room.

He had entered so quietly and shut the door as quietly, not waiting for any summons. His expression was just as grim, though he stared above her at King Robert as if he didn't want to look at her.

"I gave her the potion and she slept until that night."

"*Oui*, I finally awoke and tried to run away. If Conall hadn't come after me, I would have been torn apart by wolves—"

"*Wolves*, Campbell?"

"Aye, my lord king."

Lisette echoed his terse words with a bob of her head, finding the courage at last to look up at King Robert, only to find him staring with sternness at Conall.

"Didna you think that she might try tae escape, man?"

"Aye, I expected as much—"

"I only ran because that's what Isabeau would have done," Lisette blurted, her remorse near choking her. "I needed him to believe I was Isabeau. I didn't know what he would do with me if he knew the truth. Leave me in the woods? Take me back to Dumfries? Isabeau hates me, her bastard half-sister! She would have married me off to one of Euan MacCulloch's men—so I was to be wed either way. Yet I hoped with Conall I would have a chance at a new life. I had prayed for a miracle to free me from Isabeau and her cruelty—oh, God, please forgive me for deceiving you..."

Lisette's voice broke and she couldn't go on, fresh tears coursing down her face as she crumpled at the king's feet and pressed her forehead to the cold stone floor.

She heard a heavy sigh—King Robert?

She heard a low curse—Conall?

Then nothing for a long moment until she felt a strong pair of hands lift her to her feet, the king standing in front of her.

His face no longer forbidding, though his gaze held deep concern as he glanced beyond her to where Conall stood, silent.

"Mayhap it is me that should ask for forgiveness... from both of you. In my bitterness over my brothers' execution, I sought revenge and mayhap have condemned you tae lifelong misery, I see that now. You, Lisette, an innocent, and Conall...well, he told me quite plainly that he didna want a bride—och, even kings can be fools."

With great care and gentleness, King Robert led her to a chair and helped her to sit, Lisette murmuring her thanks. She did not allow her gaze to stray from him, not wanting to see the hatred in Conall's eyes for her deception.

If he had known the truth before their wedding, he wouldn't have wed her, she knew it as surely as she breathed.

She had heard him say, too, he didn't wish to marry anyone. Yet they were husband and wife, though she was certain the king had the power to seek an annulment for them if he wished to break them apart—

"So you prayed for a miracle, Lisette."

She met the king's gaze, his brow knit deeply as if in thought, and nodded.

"Do you see your marriage tae my baron as the answer tae your prayer? Answer carefully, lass, for much rides upon what you say."

"*Oui*, my lord, I have never felt such gladness as when I became Laird Campbell's wife," Lisette replied with all sincerity, still not daring to glance at Conall.

"Please don't send me back to my half-sister, I beg you—"

"Och, you'll not be heading south, lass, but northward tae your new home," King Robert said gruffly as if the sudden desperation in Lisette's voice and her eyes welling with tears had moved him. "I willna go against a miracle from heaven and neither will you, Campbell. Do you hear me?"

A brusque nod from Conall was his only answer, Lisette swallowing hard as he fixed his gaze upon her. A darkened gaze filled with an emotion she could not name, making her heart pound as the king gestured for Conall to come forward.

"Tae my mind, you can count yourself fortunate that it was *this* lass you abducted and not Isabeau from the sound of it. Your brother Cameron and Gabriel Mac-Lachlan have both been blessed with wives of great beauty, cleverness, and courage, and so, it seems, have you. I only hope you realize it before you think tae do anything reckless—och, we'll speak of it later, man. Take her hand."

Lisette jumped as Conall obliged him and clasped her hand in his, his callused fingers strong and warm and gripping hers tightly. So tight that she winced, but the king seemed not to have noticed—or mayhap, chose to ignore it.

"You bedded her, too, aye? Just as I commanded?"

"Aye, my lord king."

The huskiness in Conall's voice made Lisette blush to her scalp, but King Robert appeared to ignore this reaction as well.

"Then I reward you with a castle and lands in Argyllshire befitting your status as baron and as one of the men who saved my life a month past—och, I dinna like tae think upon how close I came tae feeling the executioner's blade. Has your husband told you of his bravery that night, lass?"

"She knows little of me other than as her captor," Conall interjected, his voice tinged with bitterness that made Lisette glance up at him. "Once she hears more, mayhap she will believe our marriage a curse rather than a blessing from heaven—"

"Enough, Campbell, I said we'd talk later, though I see you must hear it now! I owe you much, but you've become a man of considerable means with a wife and estate—and I demand the maturity that accompanies such responsibility. Your days of frivolous dalliances are over! Do you understand me?"

Lisette winced again at how tightly Conall's fingers grasped hers, the king's rebuke not uttered with a roar but a voice so low and vehement that she shivered.

As Conall uttered a blunt "Aye," she felt her heart sink at what King Robert had implied.

Frivolous dalliances.

She was not so naïve about the ways of men to have thought Conall hadn't enjoyed the company of women —ah God, his lovemaking the night before was proof enough!

Yet to her, it sounded as if he was well known for such liaisons, and clearly the king did not approve now that he was married. Was that why Conall hadn't wanted to wed? Mayhap he preferred a freer life than that of hearth and home and family—

"Good, we're done here," King Robert's voice broke into her racing thoughts. "Join me now for some supper and we'll drink a toast tae your marriage. Come."

Lisette could but hasten alongside Conall as they followed the king, who threw open the door and strode out into the great hall. At once cheers filled the air, while she stared in wonder at the commotion his appearance had inspired.

Warriors and courtiers alike lifted their cups to King Robert, who acknowledged them with a wave of his arm as he took his place on a raised dais. Another moment and she and Conall were seated to one side of him while serving women rushed forth to attend to them.

Or...she should say, to attend to the king and Conall. Not a one of the pretty young women spared her a glance, but were fairly shoving each other to fill their cups with ale and spear the choicest cuts of roasted meat for their plates from heaping platters. Sitting between King Robert and Conall, she might have been invisible, her cup left empty.

"A toast tae Laird and Lady Campbell, wed only yesterday!" shouted the king. Everyone echoed him and raised their cups, their felicitations and well wishes grown quite deafening.

Yet not so loud that Lisette couldn't hear two serving maids tittering behind her after one of them, comely and light-haired, had pressed between her and Conall to finally pour her some ale.

"Aye, his new wife is lovely enough...but he'll leave her tonight and find his way tae my bed just like he did when last he was here, you wait and see!"

"Mayhap he'll have enough left in him tae visit me again, too—"

"He did not!"

"Oh, aye, he did!" retorted the one with dark brown curls, her breasts nearly spilling from her tight bodice. "Do you think you're enough woman for such a man? Ha!"

Lisette felt she couldn't breathe as the two hastened away, arguing and jostling each other while Conall leaned over to say something to King Robert, his voice too low for her to hear. Then he rose abruptly from the table and without saying a word, left her sitting there.

Dear God, was he following after those two women for some carnal tryst even after what King Robert had demanded of him? Her mouth gone dry, she brought the cup to her lips with trembling fingers.

Fool! Did she think because their marriage had brought *her* such joy that Conall felt the same now that he had bedded her? They were strangers to each other no matter what they had shared last night—which hadn't been sharing at all, but an obligation ordered by the king!

Lisette felt so sick at heart for the dream she had begun to nurse that mayhap one day Conall might even grow to love her, that she could barely swallow her sip of ale. She set down the cup and stared blankly at the meat and buttered bread upon her plate, filled without her even noticing for the anguish roiling inside her.

"Dinna despair, lass—aye, it's written as plain as daylight upon your face."

Lisette gasped and met King Robert's eyes, his expression concerned as he leaned toward her.

"Do you think your husband dishonorable for what you've heard today? The reprimand I gave him? Those two lasses and their silly boasting?"

Not surprised that the king had overheard the serving maids, which meant Conall must have heard them, too, Lisette sighed heavily and shook her head.

"Not dishonorable, my lord. He's a man like any other—"

"Ah, but there you're wrong. He's as courageous and formidable a warrior as any I've known...and usually of far better humor than you've probably seen him, aye?"

She nodded, remembering with a pang the few times she had seen him smile—but why wouldn't his usual nature have suffered for having a bride foisted upon him? She almost had it in her mind to ask the king about an annulment, but his sudden chuckling made her look at him in surprise.

"Did you think Conall followed after those lasses tae seek some pleasure? Their words outraged him...a very good sign, Lady Campbell, and one that gives me great hope for your marriage. He went tae tell them not tae speak of such things anywhere near you again—ah, here he comes now."

Lisette sucked in her breath and looked beyond the dais to see Conall striding back toward them, so tall and strong and handsome. Even from halfway across the hall, she could see in the torchlight that he stared right at her, making her heart skip a beat.

"There, you see how he looks at you?" King Robert continued, chuckling again. "He might harbor some anger for a time that you deceived him, but he abducted *you* after all. You should be the angry one—och, what a curious twist of events and he hasna even admitted tae himself yet what has changed."

"Changed?" she murmured, a blush burning her cheeks that Conall had quickened his step as if in a hurry to reach her.

"Aye, I dinna feel such a brute now for setting the course that brought you together. He cares for you, lass, dinna you see it?"

Lisette did, though she could scarcely dare to believe it as Conall sat down beside her and reached for his ale cup, not uttering a word to her...which only made King Robert give a short laugh and pick up his own cup.

"Eat, the two of you—drink. Dawn will come quickly enough for your journey north. The castle is full tae bursting so I've no bedchamber tae offer you. You'll sleep with your men in the barracks, Campbell, while your lady will take a cot in the chapel with some courtiers' wives. A night's absence from each other is not so terrible a thing, aye?"

Lisette didn't say a word, though she shivered at the look Conall threw her...dark and angry and something else, much as he had looked at her last night.

Hungry...and not for food, even though he had clearly not forgiven her. Dear God, would he ever?

She prayed then and there for a blessing upon their

marriage and that one day she might see another side of Conall—the side King Robert had remarked upon and that filled her heart with longing.

Her husband laughing and smiling, how wondrous that would be!

Conall might not be pleased to have wed her, he had made that plain enough even last night. Yet she vowed to herself that she would do her best to make him a good and faithful wife, truly the only thing she could offer him.

That, and mayhap children...hope filling her that it would be so.

CHAPTER 10

"Blast and damn, Conall! Did you have tae ride so hard tae reach us that your new bride couldna lift her head for exhaustion?"

Conall ignored Cameron and took another draft of ale, though he did feel remorse for pushing himself and his men—and Lisette—so relentlessly since leaving Dumbarton yesterday morning.

Now it was late afternoon. The great hall of Campbell Castle, his brother's fortress, empty but for a few servants wiping down trestle tables and arranging wooden benches in preparation for the evening meal.

A smoldering log fell through the iron grate in the fireplace, which was massive to warm the cavernous hall. Conall stared at the glowing sparks spiraling upward that reminded him of the lustrous red glints in Lisette's hair, and then thrust the thought away as he sank deeper into the chair next to his brother's.

Weariness overwhelmed him, too, but he wasn't ready to retire to the bedchamber where Cameron's Irish bride of only a few weeks, Aislinn, had escorted Lisette. Conall had said he would carry her up into the tower, but his flame-haired sister-in-law had insisted brusquely that a manservant would help her, her vivid blue eyes flashing fire at Conall.

Aye, she'd been angry to see Lisette's exhausted state, while Cameron had held his tongue as Conall had apprised him of the last week's events. Och, had it been only a week since King Robert had told him he must ride to Dumfries to steal Euan MacCulloch's intended bride, Isabeau, from under his nose?

Conall had stolen her all right, the wrong woman who was now his wife! Not Isabeau at all, but Lisette Mathilde Charpentier.

Calling herself *Lisette Isabeau* had only been a ruse she had concocted right there in the very church where they had wed, lying to him through her teeth. Had it been a lie as well when she told the king that she hadn't known such gladness as when she and Conall had married? She had certainly seemed giddy with joy, which probably angered him the most.

Even more than her half-hearted attempt to run into the woods—another ruse!—that had brought wolves down upon them.

Even more than lying to him, as he suspected, about Euan MacCulloch giving her a vial of lilac perfume, which must be her half-sister's favorite scent for how the room at the convent had reeked of it.

Och, Lisette had been giddy because her plan to deceive him had worked, so why wouldn't she be elated?

Yet he could have avoided a wedding altogether if she had only told him the truth. He would never have left her in the woods—though he might have returned her to Dumfries and tried to abduct the *real* Isabeau a second time. Foolhardy, most likely, for by then the element of surprise was long gone and MacCulloch's guards no doubt encircling the convent, but at least, again, Conall wouldn't have been wed.

To the most beautiful, sweet-tempered woman he had ever known, his conflicting thoughts held captive by Lisette.

"You're scowling, brother."

Conall met Cameron's gaze, blurting in frustration, "How can I not? Whenever I think of all her lies, I should despise Lisette for her trickery. I dinna want a bride—"

"So you've said many times."

"Aye, and I could have avoided the plague of it all if she'd only told me the truth."

"What then? You would have returned her tae a life of misery and a half-sister's cruelty? That's not the brother I know—but mayhap, I dinna really know you after all. I always believed us as close as two brothers can be, yet I dinna recognize this Conall. Aye, fierceness upon the battlefield is one thing, but all of this scowling? Your good humor fled? No laughter? No light-hearted jests?"

"Marriage is no lighthearted matter, at least not for me. You're right, you dinna know me, Cameron."

Conall turned back to the fire and took another draught of ale, but the brew was tasteless in his mouth.

Aye, something was wrong with him.

His life turned upside down by a king's command and deceit from a lass who looked as innocent as a fawn and had the sweetest voice he'd ever heard.

Yet it was her eyes...her soft brown eyes looking at him with such trust and tenderness in spite of how brusquely he had treated her since they left Dumbarton Castle, making him feel disgusted with himself. With a vehement curse he flung the rest of his ale into the flames, which hissed and sputtered and flared higher, causing Cameron to utter a low whistle.

A low whistle much like Conall had done when he had seen his painfully shy brother at Aislinn's bedside after she'd been found barely alive in the fortress prison —aye, tending to her so carefully and never taking his eyes from her.

"*What?*" Bristling, Conall glared at Cameron for he knew exactly what his brother was thinking.

That he, too, might have finally met a woman that moved him to act unlike he ever had before...but Cameron didn't know anything about Lorna. Conall had loved her and yet she had left him, though strangely, the memory now didn't cut him quite as deep—

"Did you bother tae ask Lisette about her life in France, Conall?"

He bristled again, shaking his head. "We hardly spoke. How could we when surrounded by my own men and the twenty-odd warriors King Robert sent with me tae train with your fighters before we make our way tae my estate? We were never alone."

"Ah, then, you'll have much tae talk about with your bride. I would think you curious tae learn why she was so desperate tae escape her half-sister that she would wed a stranger. The very man who forced a sleeping elixir upon her and ruthlessly abducted her. You may see it as deceit—but I see it as brave beyond measure. She knows as little about you as you know about her. Mayhap this week when you're not training your new men and she's had a chance tae rest and regain her strength, you might spend some time with her. Aye, make her laugh and chase away those dark smudges under her eyes—"

"*Are you done, Cameron?*"

Conall had thrust himself up from his chair and stared down at his brother, who didn't appear perturbed at all by his angry roar.

Instead, Cameron gave another low whistle, which made Conall turn on his heel and stride from the hall... though in truth, he was already thinking about Lisette, his heart thudding faster.

He had seen those smudges, too, which made concern flare deep inside him.

He was a brute! Callous and unfeeling to have not taken more care with her and slowed their pace, even a little.

The few times they had paused to rest and water the horses had been brief, their longest stop no more than a couple hours when she had slumped at the base of a tree and fallen asleep, too weary even to eat an oatcake. He had wrapped her woolen cloak more snugly around her, the night air chill and tinged with a fine mist—*och, what had he done to her?*

Conall took the stone steps of the tower three at a time, almost careening into Aislinn at the top. Yet instead of stepping aside, she blocked him with her body and pushed against his chest with splayed hands.

"Where do you think you're going, Conall Campbell?"

Her tone fierce, he didn't attempt to shove past her, though he did wrap his fingers tightly around the hilt of his sword.

He hadn't forgotten how she had pulled Cameron's sword from his belt and tried to strike him down, a woman warrior through and through and mayhap the very moment when she had won his brother's heart.

"My wife. Does she sleep?"

"Aye, finally, the poor lassie. If you're planning to wake her by climbing into bed with her, shame on you, Conall! She's pale as a phantom and needs rest, not her new husband demanding his way with her."

"Is that why you think...?" Conall didn't finish, for how else would Aislinn judge him from the behavior he had displayed in the past with women? As if reading his mind, she dropped her hands that had balled into fists.

"I'm the lady of Campbell Castle now, and I'll send any serving maid packing who dares so much as to glance sideways at you, do you hear me? So don't be thinking you'll find comfort elsewhere while *your* lady wife is trying to mend from all she's gone through. An abduction! A sleeping potion! A wedding and bedding—"

"All ordered by the king," Conall said tightly,

though still he did not try to push past her for the indignation blazing in her eyes, aye, not if he didn't want to find himself shoved down the steps. "She would have been spared the last two if she'd not deceived me —*och*!"

Aislinn had shoved him now, Conall saving himself from tumbling backward by grabbing the wall. She gasped, too, and caught his arm to help steady him, her lovely features lit by chagrin as she shook her head.

"Oh, Conall, forgive me, but you should know better than to vex a red-haired Irishwoman. I'm just so angry with you."

"Truly? I couldna tell." He found himself chuckling, which made Aislinn pull him with her into the hallway, her expression once again grown serious.

"I hope you're not going to wake her. She's so sweet a young woman and as yielding as a lamb. How could anyone hurt her so? Her half-sister, her stepmother— though that wretched woman's gone to her grave, thank God."

"I know nothing of what you speak," Conall said with some embarrassment, remembering what Cameron had urged him in the great hall. "What hurt?"

"Years of it, since she was a babe. Lisette was exhausted, but she seemed to want to talk to me so I sat by the bed and listened. Her mother was a kitchen maid and beloved by Lisette's father, but she died in childbirth. So her father brought Lisette into the house and that's when the misery started. He did his best to protect her, but after he died last year, things only grew worse. You may fault her for not revealing that she wasn't Isabeau, and she wept in the telling of how she deceived you—"

"She wept?" Conall felt his throat tighten as Aislinn nodded and rushed on.

"Aye, so sorrowfully that I wept, too, and the serving maids that helped me to bathe her and brush her hair and dress her for bed. She's so lovely, Conall, but I fear not as strong as you mayhap thought her."

"God help me, does a healer need tae see her?"

"Tobias has already come and gone. Too much has happened to her too quickly, the course of her life changed almost overnight, to my mind. He agreed that a few days' rest was the best balm for her."

Relief coursed through Conall, so furious with himself now that he felt close to choking upon it as Aislinn laid her hand on his arm.

"You're a brother to me now, so I won't hold anything back from you. Lisette told me that if you decide to seek an annulment from the Church, no matter King Robert bade you to accept the marriage, she will not raise her voice against it. She fears that mayhap you hate her—"

"*Hate her*?" Now Conall leaned his back against the wall and lowered his head. "Aye, I can see how she would think that of me. I hardly spoke tae her after we left Dumbarton and have showed her little else but anger..." Sighing heavily, he raised his eyes to look at Aislinn. "I swear tae you and Cameron that I dinna hate her. She's my wife, though she surely deserves better. I wanted *never* tae wed, but I willna have the lass weeping because she believes I dinna want her."

"So no annulment?"

Aislinn had whispered, as if she couldn't believe what Conall had just said, while he shook his head.

"No annulment."

"Then swear to me one more thing, that you won't break her heart. She's so kind, thinking only of you. She even said that if you choose to seek the company of other women, she will try to understand because she doesn't wish you unhappiness—"

"Oh, God." Conall drew in a long breath and exhaled slowly, the weight of Aislinn's words striking him like a sword blow.

He had never known a humbler moment...or one more damning.

Frivolous dalliances, aye, that's what King Robert had called them, and Conall could only agree.

Everything he'd done had been to forget Lorna. Yet now, strangely, he was hard-pressed to remember exactly what she had looked like as a vision of soft brown eyes filled with tears tore at him.

"Those days are behind me, Aislinn, I swear it, as God is my witness. Will you allow me a moment tae see her?"

She didn't answer, only stared at him for a long moment in astonishment, until at last she nodded.

"Aye, Conall, but don't wake her...please."

She gestured to a closed door halfway down the hall, but she didn't move to accompany him.

Instead she turned and hastened down the steps in a swirl of green silk while Conall went in the opposite direction, his heart thudding hard again.

He didn't want to wake Lisette, either, only to look in upon her. He opened the door and slipped into the candlelit room without a sound, his breath caught now as he moved to the curtained bed.

Dressed in a white long-sleeved nightgown, she lay motionless on her side with one hand balled under her chin like a child's, her other hand dangling from the bed. He longed to reach out and tuck those slender fingers within his own to feel their warmth and assure himself that all was well—but all wasn't well.

Not with Lisette thinking that he might wish to seek an annulment and that he hated her and desired to share the beds of other women.

He could see the wetness staining her pillow from her tears, Conall truly despising himself at that moment for the distress he had caused her.

He vowed to himself, too, that he would do better—

he *must* do better. What kind of man would that make him if he didn't?

In her sleep, Lisette suddenly sighed...a ragged sound telling him that her dream might be just as cold and bleak as life seemed to her now. It was all he could do not to lean down and touch her cheek to comfort her, but somehow he refrained and moved away from the bed.

Another moment more and he had left the room and closed the door behind him...not seeing her stir and lift her head.

~

"Conall?"

Lisette blinked open her eyelids, still heavy and swollen from weeping.

Something had pulled her out of a dream...a slow intake of breath, a creak of the wooden floor, but she saw nothing and dropped her head back onto the pillow.

Yet she smelled the masculine scent of him hanging in the air—sweat and wood fire and horses, and knew in her heart that he had just been there.

Yet why hadn't he stayed? It wasn't night, but surely he must be tired from their journey and needed sleep, too. Was there something else he must do first? Someone else he must see?

That thought brought such a pang that tears welled again, hot and stinging though she did her best to force them back.

She had told Aislinn, her new sister-in-law, that she would try to understand if Conall sought the warmth of another woman's arms—but she had lied!

She had never been one to utter falsehoods even in the worst times with Isabeau and Claudia and now they seemed to tumble from her lips.

She didn't want Conall to seek an annulment!

She didn't want him to seek solace from other women when he had a warm and willing wife in his bed!

After Conall had been so distant toward her since leaving Douglas Castle, her flagging hope had made her say those things in the first place, but she hadn't meant them! All she wanted was for them to find happiness together and for him one day to love her—heaven above, was that too much of a miracle to hope for?

Just as Lisette knew she had fallen in love with him from the moment he'd claimed her, the ache only growing in her heart.

CHAPTER 11

"You look so pretty, Lisette. Are you feeling better this morning?"

Lisette nodded at the thirteen-year-old girl standing off to one side while two seamstresses finished stitching the hem on the lavender silk gown she had donned.

Sunlight spilled through the window upon a half dozen gowns in as many hues laid out upon the bed, and brightened Sorcha's long hair to an even blonder shade—if that was possible.

Cameron and Aislinn's adopted daughter might think her pretty, but Lisette had never seen anyone as beautiful as Sorcha Campbell with her flawless skin and luminous blue eyes. From the moment the girl had shyly entered her room yesterday with Aislinn, Lisette had felt drawn to her, and she reached out her hand.

At once Sorcha rushed forward to squeeze her fingers and gift her with a smile that seemed to light up the room even more than the brilliant sunshine.

"Aislinn says you're strong enough now tae take a walk with me. We have a lovely garden and I'll show you my chicken coop, too! Daran built it for me, Aislinn's brother, but he's gone tae train at MacLachlan Castle for a week or two. I asked him tae make it nice and big for lots of chickens, and he did!"

Inspired by the girl's excitement, Lisette smiled back, though to do so felt strange to her.

She had smiled so little these past three days during which she had slept mostly and spent the rest of her time standing at the window that overlooked the bailey, watching Conall train with his men.

He hadn't come to see her once, other than that afternoon when she had sworn he had stood beside the bed, though she knew Aislinn had asked him not to visit so Lisette could regain her strength.

It amazed her still that the hard-paced journey had cost her so dearly. Yet mayhap it was just as Aislinn had surmised—that everything Lisette had experienced from the abduction to her marriage to arriving at Campbell Castle had proved too much for her, both in body and her emotions.

She had to agree, but she did feel much better and was anxious to finally take a walk outside. Sorcha had let go of her hand and waited by the door while the seamstresses rose from their knees, having finished hemming her gown.

Both of the women from the village outside the fortress gates appeared quite pleased with their handiwork, and Lisette murmured her thanks. They had hastily sewn her new wardrobe at Aislinn's request, her sister-in-law's kindness and generosity filling her with gratitude.

Lisette couldn't have been more comfortable in this sumptuous suite of rooms, which had once belonged to Conall and Cameron's first cousin, Cora, who had been married to Earl Seoras MacDougall. Lisette had heard from Aislinn all about that cruel man and his misdeeds and of Cora's unhappiness as his wife.

The young widow had left the fortress to return to her parents' home in north Argyll a few days after her husband had been slain by Gabriel MacLachlan, who along with Cameron and Conall had saved King

Robert's life. It made Lisette shudder to think that so great a man had come close to meeting an untimely end here, the ringing sound of swords upon swords drawing her to the window.

Holding her breath, she searched the men training so vigorously below but she didn't see Conall. He usually stood at the very center of the bailey with Cameron, both of them shouting brusque commands and even demonstrating themselves how to thrust and parry. She had felt her heart seem to stop several times at how closely Conall dodged blows, his sword flashing in the sunlight.

On one occasion—truly so close a disaster that Lisette felt her face grow hot at the vivid memory—Conall had spied her at the window and seemed to have forgotten what he was doing, barely ducking a blow that might have ended his life.

She had fled back to the bed and sobbed into her pillow at the horror of it, and from then on had stood off to one side of the window where he couldn't see her.

Yet mayhap he had sensed her standing there, for Conall had glanced upward enough times that he seemed to know she was watching him—but where was he now?

"Lisette, shall we go?" Fairly dancing with impatience, Sorcha ran back to her and grabbed her hand to draw her from the room.

The girl's laughter warmed her heart since Aislinn had told her, too, of how Sorcha had tragically lost her parents and that it had taken her days before she'd smiled again—no doubt helped along by her chicken coop.

That had been earlier in the month and now no one would have known the grief Sorcha had suffered for how lighthearted she appeared to Lisette, the two of them swinging their arms as they hastened down the hall.

"Speckles is my new rooster, but you must take care," Sorcha advised her breathlessly when they reached the tower steps. "He's nicer than the one I named him after—but he'll still peck your toes right through your slippers!"

The girl's outburst of laughter was infectious, and Lisette laughed, too. She skipped with her down the steps so quickly that she felt breathless as well at the bottom, but Sorcha kept right on tugging her along.

Not until they were passing by the entrance to the great hall did Lisette hear Aislinn cry out, "Oh, Sorcha, not so fast!"

That made the girl stop and Lisette, too. She braced her hand upon a wall to catch her breath as Aislinn came rushing toward them, Conall and Cameron not far behind.

Lisette felt her heart leap to see Conall again, and she could but stare in amazement at the resemblance between him and his brother. The two formidable Highlanders in their dark tunics and plaid breacans appeared almost twins with their midnight hair and similar features, though she knew they were two years apart.

Aislinn had shared much with her about all of them while Lisette had convalesced...but not why Conall hadn't wished never to wed and she hadn't asked her. Hopefully one day she would find out such an intimate detail on her own—

"Will you run Lisette ragged and her only just out of her bedchamber?" Aislinn's voice broke into Lisette's thoughts, though her tone held more warmth than reprimand as she gave Sorcha a hug. "I told you a *walk*, sweeting. Go on ahead and lead the way while Conall accompanies her, aye, brother?"

Conall had already moved toward Lisette before Aislinn's suggestion, his gaze filled with concern as if noting her flushed cheeks and unsteady breath.

"I-I'm fine, truly," Lisette murmured, but three days of straying no further from her bed than the window had affected her stamina—either that, or she hadn't fully regained it. Before she could blink, he had wound his arm in hers and seemed to wait until she was ready, which made her blush anew with embarrassment. "Forgive me. I've always been quite sound—"

"It's the Scots weather," interjected Cameron as Aislinn slipped her hand in her husband's. "Misty mornings and cool evenings."

"Aye, and a relentless journey that no bride should have been made tae endure," Conall said in a low voice as he met Lisette's startled glance. "If anyone owes an apology, it's me tae you. Will you forgive me, Lisette?"

She nodded, too astonished to speak as Aislinn added brightly, "Well then, off with you now and enjoy your walk while the sky is clear and the air warm. My husband believes a fierce storm is brewing to the west."

"Aye, wife, as they do in midsummer—flaring up with little warning. Sorcha, grant Conall and Lisette some time tae visit alone, will you?" Cameron bade her with gruff affection in his voice. "After they've had a chance tae see your chickens, of course."

With a wave of her hand, Sorcha was already racing toward the archway leading out into the bailey, her blue tunic fluttering around her legs and her blonde hair flying.

Cameron's rich laughter echoed from the high ceiling as Lisette and Conall followed after her, but not at so rushed a pace.

"That used tae be a rare thing," he murmured as they stepped outside into the sunshine. "My brother laughing...before Aislinn, I mean. He changed for the better because of her."

Lisette said nothing for how her heartbeat quickened to have Conall so near, his arm still looped through hers, and speaking so easily to her.

His voice no longer edged with anger nor his blue eyes darkened to an ominous hue. She could but gaze up at him in wonder, wanting to pinch herself over his relaxed demeanor.

As they continued after Sorcha, who was skipping a good ways ahead of them, Conall pointed out to Lisette some of the outbuildings bordering the bailey—the blacksmith and the armory and the massive stable. Yet he could have been speaking an unknown language for all she heard him.

He changed for the better because of her.

Those were the only words that reverberated in her mind as she wondered if such a miracle might be possible with Conall—ah, God, she prayed that it would be so! A great love had been forged between Aislinn and Cameron from the trials and dangers they had faced, as well as the personal struggles they had overcome.

Cameron's affliction of painful shyness.

Aislinn's arduous quest to be recognized as a woman more than capable of making up her own mind about her future.

Was Conall beginning to look upon her as more than the unwanted bride that had been forced upon him? Mayhap a wife that could inspire him to loyalty and faithfulness? He stopped so abruptly and pulled her around to face him that Lisette gasped, his gaze burning into hers.

"Tell me you forgive me, lass, I must hear it if we're tae start anew. I know you're not tae blame for anything that's happened—aye, especially our marriage. I would have done the same if I'd been in your place—"

"If you'd been born a woman," Lisette could not help breaking in with a small smile, not sure why she'd found humor in so serious a moment, though she had. To her surprise, Conall nodded and chuckled, his expression lightening.

"Aye." Yet no sooner had he begun to smile when he

grew serious again. "Aislinn told me some of what you suffered in France...your half-sister and stepmother. I dinna fault you for claiming you were Isabeau—*Lisette* Isabeau. At least I knew your given name—och, do you remember I said it suited you better?"

"*Oui*, I remember." Conall stared at her so intently that Lisette felt as if she could scarcely breathe...something blossoming between them, she could feel it. He clasped her fingers, her hands so small within his larger grasp, and squeezed them gently, his voice filled with apology.

"I wanted tae visit you these past days, but Aislinn wouldna hear of it. She wields a sword, you know, as well as many a man. She grabbed Cameron's sword once like a wild hoyden and used it against him—aye, it's best not tae cross her."

Conall chuckled again at the remembering, which only made Lisette's heart beat faster.

"You did come to my room that first day, though. I sensed you'd been there and I called out your name."

"I didna hear it, wife, forgive me. If I had, I would have come back tae you. I swore at your bedside that I would do better by you, and I meant it. Aislinn told me that you feared mayhap I'd seek an annulment of our marriage and that I must hate you, but there will be no annulment and I *dinna* hate you."

"No annulment?" Lisette echoed, even as Conall more tightly gripped her hands.

"Never."

"A-and you don't hate me?"

"Far from it, lass, these past few days have shown me as much. You're brave and beautiful and as fine a bride as any man could hope for, however we came tae be wed. I will share with you all that I've been given by King Robert and protect you tae my dying breath, yet I willna promise you love—aye, that I canna do."

His expression had grown so hard that Lisette felt like she'd been struck, her knees feeling weak beneath her. Yet Sorcha calling out to them allowed her no more time to absorb what he'd just said as Conall laced his fingers with hers and drew her with him across the last expanse of the bailey.

Sorcha stood beside a stone wall, waving for them to hurry, which Lisette found almost impossible to do when she felt simply like crumpling to the ground.

Tears clouded her eyes, but she swallowed them back, not wanting Sorcha to think that anything was amiss.

Yet what had Lisette expected? That Conall would declare his impassioned love for her and seal it with a kiss? Berating herself again for a fool, she lifted her chin and forced a smile as they reached Sorcha, who beckoned for them to follow her.

"The garden's right through the gate! See how green and pretty? We have herbs and roses and vegetables—though I dinna care for many of them, well, except carrots. I do love tae eat carrots and sometimes a wee bit of turnip. Isn't that a funny word, turnip?"

Sorcha chattered on as she flew through the open gate and into what appeared a small Garden of Eden within the fortress walls, which astonished Lisette for all she'd heard about Earl Seoras and his penchant only for battle and bloodshed.

"Cora's garden," Conall said as if surmising her thoughts. He still held Lisette's hand, though she had no idea why. He didn't love her after all, so why be so solicitous of her?

For all she had sworn to herself that she would be a good and faithful wife, right now she didn't feel very good at all and pulled her hand away. Conall appeared surprised for an instant, but before he could reach for her again, Lisette hurried to where Sorcha was bending over a rose bush laden with crimson blooms.

"Aislinn told me these were Cora's favorite. Smell them, Lisette...mmm, so sweet."

She obliged her, the heady fragrance wonderful indeed, while Conall stood to one side and watched them. Or he did, until a rumble of thunder made him glance up at the darkening sky. The light breeze had grown stronger, too, whipping Lisette's gown around her legs.

"I think the chickens will have tae wait," he called out to them as a flash of lightning blinded Lisette and made Sorcha shriek, a flaming tree limb crashing to the ground at one corner of the garden.

Before she knew it, Conall had grabbed her hand and Sorcha's, too, and pulled both of them with him back toward the gate as the wind began to whistle around them.

A deafening crack of thunder made Sorcha scream again, and she burst into tears. "I dinna like storms! *I dinna like storms!*"

Lisette didn't like them, either, not when she was outside with nowhere to duck for shelter.

More lightning flashed too near for comfort and this time, she felt the fine hairs lifting on her arms. The same thing must have happened to Conall. His vehement curse was drowned out by another boom of thunder and now Sorcha began to sob in earnest.

"Take her!" Lisette cried out against the wind that had heightened to a bluster. "I'll follow you!"

He did, sweeping up Sorcha and running with her across the bailey as the sky opened up into a torrential downpour.

Lisette scurried after them only to stumble and fall to her knees, crying out at a sharp pain in her ankle. She managed to stand up, but the storm had become a raging tempest with deafening thunder that shook the ground.

She could barely see for the lashing rain that stung

her face like nettles, the dirt becoming mud that sucked at her slippers.

Another blinding flash of lightning made her scream and limp back to the wall surrounding the garden, where she huddled and pressed her cheek against the cold stones.

"Conall...God help me! *Conall*!"

CHAPTER 12

"*Lisette*!"

For a heart-stopping moment, Conall didn't see her for the cold rain stinging his eyes, until Cameron, running alongside him, shouted in his ear.

"There, by the wall!"

Conall breathed a prayer of thanks, but she looked so small and helpless crouching near the ground with her sodden lavender gown blending into the gray stones.

He called her name again, but she clearly couldn't hear him over the howling wind. She didn't lift her head until he stood over her and reached down to pull her into his arms, Lisette blinking against the driving rain.

"Oh, Conall...I couldn't follow you, my ankle—"

"Shh, lass, I've got you." Conall swept her up and held her close, Cameron clapping him on the back and then sprinting alongside him as they splashed through rivulets of water and mud to reach the keep.

Aislinn awaited them at the entranceway, Sorcha still hiccoughing with tears and holding onto her while serving women rushed forward with armloads of towels.

"Take her into the hall where the fire is stoked and blazing!" Aislinn shouted over another clap of thunder, but Conall shook his head. Lisette shivered so fiercely against him that he feared for her, a glance at her ashen pallor and bluish lips, her wet hair plastered to her head, making him move instead for the tower steps.

"Follow him, *go!*" came Cameron's roared command, Conall glancing over his shoulder to see three maidservants hurrying after him while his brother shook water from himself and took a towel from his wife.

Cameron would be fine, and Sorcha, too, with Aislinn tending after them—but Lisette? As Conall raced up the steps, nearly slipping for the water dripping from him, his concern for her only mounted when she began to shiver even more violently.

"We're almost there, lass—almost there," he murmured against her wet hair.

He shivered, too, though he had faced worse on the battlefield when there had been no shelter from thunderstorms at all other than a sodden breacan over his head. He kicked open the door to their chamber, making Lisette gasp, and strode inside, roaring out commands to the maidservants hard on his heels.

"Stoke the fire! Pull back the covers on the bed!"

A flurry of commotion surrounded them as Conall set Lisette down on her feet in front of the fireplace. Without any more delay, he reached down to grab the hem of her wet tunic and pulled the garment over her head.

Logs crackled and flared into a bright warming blaze at the prodding of a stout serving maid with an iron poker, while the other two rushed forward with towels, only to have Conall grab them from their hands. It was him that swiftly dried Lisette from her head to her toes while doing his best to focus upon his task though she stood there naked and shaking.

Her beautiful body limned in firelight and her widened eyes never straying from his face, Conall swallowing hard that he would feel his lower body tighten with desire at such a dire moment.

Her lips still blue and her teeth chattering, but she shivered less, thankfully, Conall accepting a woolen blanket pulled from the armoire by one of the women to wrap around Lisette. Only then did he sweep her up again and deposit her upon the bed where he covered her with more blankets tucked up to her chin.

"M-my thanks, h-h-husband," came her broken whisper, but Conall only nodded and went back to the fireplace where he picked up the poker and prodded the flames into an even hotter blaze. A knock upon the open door made him turn around to see a serving maid bearing a tray laden with steaming cups and bowls, his own silent thanks going out to Aislinn.

"Chicken broth, Laird Campbell...and warm cider."

"Set it upon the table by the bed," he said tersely, anxious for the servants to leave them in peace so he could strip out of his own wet clothes. As if guessing his thoughts, several of them gestured to the towels stacked upon a chair and then hurried from the room, the last maidservant closing the door with a thud behind her.

No sound now but the rain beating upon the window, the crackling of the flames, and Conall's hard breathing, for he had not stopped yet for a moment to tend to himself.

"Conall...please. You're still dripping wet..."

Lisette's eyes wide and pleading as if she feared for him, he set to the task of swiftly undressing and toweling himself dry, leaving his damp hair ruffled and covering his face.

To his surprise, he heard a soft laugh from the bed, his gaze meeting Lisette's after he had swept his hair out of his eyes.

To his relief, her color was much improved and not anywhere near as pale, though he could see that she still shivered. Within three strides, he had joined her in the bed and burrowed next to her beneath the covers, Conall pulling her against him to warm her.

A good thing, too, for her skin felt cold and made his flesh pucker with goosebumps. She pressed closer still as if craving the heat of his body, a sigh escaping her that evidenced her own relief.

"It was good tae hear you laugh, lass," he murmured against her hair, thankfully drying from the heat in the room. At any other time he might have felt the warmth stifling, but now he was more than grateful for the dancing flames in the fireplace as her shivering began to ease. "Would you like some broth?"

"Not yet, stay with me," came her whisper against his chest, making his skin pucker again, but this time not because her flesh was cold. "You did look funny with your hair so wild and tousled...like a boy's."

He could sense that she smiled, though he couldn't see her face with Lisette snuggled against him. Her body felt warmer now and so willowy in his arms, which made him grimace and press his head into the pillow— och, was he a rutting beast to desire her so intensely when she was still recovering from this most recent scare?

"You saved me again," she murmured, pressing her lips to where his heart thrummed faster to have her so near. The sweet tenderness of her kiss moved him more deeply than he could have ever imagined...and made him swallow hard to feel such fierce emotion, Conall drawing her even closer.

"I told you that I'd protect you tae my dying breath," he murmured back, caressing the silkiness of her skin beneath the covers. "You gave me a fright when I couldna see you through the rain—och, it's done now. Try tae rest, Lisette..."

She nodded against his chest, even that small movement making Conall clench his jaw and stare up at the brocade canopy above them—as if he could rest, too!

The last few nights spent apart from her had left him craving her presence, her nearness, the scent of her, the feel of her, though he had told himself that it was only the desire of a man for his wife. Yet something else stirred within him now for this woman who had been thrust into his life—aye, through no fault of her own!

When he had faced her in the bailey and told her that he couldn't promise her love, he had known he lied, the wounded look in her eyes making him regret the words as soon as he'd uttered them. Yet he had immediately hardened himself and stifled again the war raging inside him that seemed to intensify with each passing day.

He didn't want to love Lisette! Such emotion only brought heartache and pain—och, how many times now had he come close to losing her?

A sleeping elixir that might have caused her never to awake.

Snarling wolves.

A harsh and unrelenting journey that had left her weak and exhausted.

Now a thunderstorm with deadly lightning striking all around them—the flaming tree limb in the garden like a sign from heaven that some sinister force yearned to claim her.

What might happen on that day when he wasn't there to help her? Protect her? Och, to think of it made Conall hug Lisette so tightly she roused from the sleepiness that had descended upon her and gasped, though at once he lowered his head to kiss her cheek and soothe her.

"Forgive me, wife...rest now."

She nodded again and sighed so deeply as if comforted by the warmth of their bodies pressed together... or mayhap it was simply because he held her in his arms.

Cradling her. Kissing her forehead, the tip of her nose, and her closed eyelids as that same intense feeling overwhelmed him.

No simple stirring, but something as bright and hot

as the flames lighting the room...God help him, he was lost.

~

Lisette flickered open her eyes and tried to stretch out her arms, but she was tucked so securely beneath the covers that she could hardly move.

Only then, with a glance around her, did she realize she was alone, but not for long. She heard a rap at the door and whoever wanted entrance didn't wait for a response, Sorcha bursting into the room and running up to the bed.

"Oh, Lisette, did you see that wicked lightning in the garden? Cora's apple tree, too. Now that the rain has stopped, Aislinn sent some servants out straight-away tae gather the fallen apples tae make tarts for tonight's supper—"

"Have you seen Conall?"

Sorcha suddenly looked a bit downcast that Lisette hadn't seemed interested about the apple tree, and then shrugged.

"He left with Cameron and a host of men a few hours ago. There's flooding in the village from all the rain, but I'm sure everything's fine now. Look! The clouds are gone."

Indeed the sky had cleared, Lisette guessing that it must be past midday from the angle of the sun's rays cascading through the window. Again, Sorcha appeared as ethereal as an angel with her blonde hair framing her face, but she had an impish smile that looked anything but heavenly.

"I know a secret...but Aislinn made me promise not tae tell. It's a surprise for you and Conall—"

"*Sorcha...*"

At the sound of Aislinn's voice, the girl clapped her hand over her mouth and twisted around even as

Lisette tried again to extricate herself from the covers. She had slept so soundly that she hadn't felt Conall climb from the bed, an intense yearning for his closeness overwhelming her as Aislinn retrieved a nightgown from the armoire and then rushed forward to help her.

"Your husband couldn't have pulled those covers more tightly, aye? You've been snug and warm, though, which I'm sure was his aim since he couldn't remain here with you. He wasn't too happy to leave with Cameron—but I assured him that I would check on you. I've come and gone twice before now, but you were sleeping so peacefully. Was it my sweeting that woke you?"

"*Non*, I was already awake," Lisette murmured, the covers thrown back so she was able at last to sit up and pull the nightgown over her head.

She blushed that Aislinn and Sorcha had seen her nakedness, but Aislinn merely took her hand to assist her as she swung her legs to the floor. The moment she put weight on her feet, though, she winced, and sank right back down on the bed.

"Oh, aye, Conall told me that you might have twisted your ankle," Aislinn said with concern in her eyes. "Sorcha, run and call for the healer, will you?"

At once the girl bobbed her head and rushed from the room while Lisette sighed and reached down to massage her right foot. "It doesn't hurt as much now, though it is sore."

"Tobias will know exactly what to do, but your ankle doesn't appear bruised, a good thing. You've not had an easy time of it since you arrived at Campbell Castle, but I hope the next few days will be happier for you, Lisette."

At the apology in Aislinn's voice, she looked up in surprise and reached out to squeeze her hand. "You've been so kind to me, so gracious. I can never thank you enough, truly. You and your husband and Sorcha—"

"Aye, it's been our pleasure, but I'll be happier, too, once Conall sees what's as plain as the nose upon his face. He's besotted with you, though I doubt he would ever admit it. Not yet, anyway. These Scots Highlanders are the most stubborn men on God's earth, and so reluctant to admit to any hidden pain. Cameron's was his terrible shyness since boyhood. When first we met, he could hardly look me in the eye, let alone speak to me. Conall was the one who told me about his brother's affliction, but it's a mystery about what's made Conall so unwilling to open his heart...though he has begun to done so, Lisette, to you. Do you not see it?"

CHAPTER 12

Lisette felt her heart beating so hard that she could only gape at Aislinn, the astonishing words having tumbled from the beautiful young Irishwoman in a rush.

The next instant brought a soft laugh from Aislinn, who shook her head.

"The two of you as blind to love as can be—ah, but these matters of the heart must find their own way, as they did for Cameron and me. I never dreamed when I came to Scotland to fight for King Robert that one of his most renowned warriors would become my husband, a true blessing from heaven. Your marriage to Conall is a blessing, too, and I pray it's not long before you both admit to it. Did he tell you he has no intention of seeking an annulment?"

Lisette nodded, still so stunned that her voice sounded more a croak when finally she spoke. *"Oui,* he said as much on our way to the garden. He told me, too, that he didn't hate me—"

"A double-edged sword, hatred and love! Of course he doesn't hate you, Lisette, he cares deeply for you."

"Non, he said he could not promise me love. I've been hoping and praying since we wed that one day, it

might be different and he grow to feel as I do..." Lisette fell silent, her face burning at what she had just revealed, even as a smile spread across Aislinn's face.

"So you have fallen in love with your handsome Highlander...just as I did with Cameron. I'll not speak a word of it to Conall, I promise, Lisette—but you can answer me now, aye? Do you not see from the way he looks at you that he's falling in love with you, too? I've never seen him so stricken as when he carried you out of the storm. Ah, God, and when I forbade him to visit you these past days so you could rest, I knew he wanted to defy me. He's not sleeping and scarcely eating and all the while training his men until they're ready to collapse from exhaustion—"

"*Mon Dieu*, is it truly possible?" Her heart clamoring in her breast, Lisette felt her eyes welling as she glanced out the window and wished desperately that Conall would return to her.

You gave me a fright when I couldna see you through the rain...

So he had said right after she had kissed the spot above his heart, so grateful that he had braved the raging thunderstorm to find her.

So grateful for the warmth of his body chasing away the chill of her own, the length of him hard and muscled while she snuggled naked in his arms, her shivering faded.

She had felt so safe and protected as drowsiness overcame her until he hugged her so fiercely that she started...though his tender kisses soon lulled her into a deep slumber.

Would a man who could not promise love have held her so close and caressed her to sleep? Lisette turned back from the window to find Aislinn studying her with a look of such kindness and understanding that fresh tears blurred her eyes.

"Give Conall some time, sister—we are sisters now to each other, after all. I told him what you'd said about trying to understand if he sought the comfort of other women, but that brought his most vehement response of all. He vowed to me that those wanton days were behind him, as God was his witness, and I believe him—"

"Frivolous dalliances...that's what King Robert called them," Lisette broke in softly, remembering the sternness in the man's voice. "I felt then I had done a terrible thing to Conall to wed him when mayhap he prefers a life so much different than anything I could offer him. I saw at supper that night how the serving women shoved and pushed each other to get closer to him and fill his cup, his plate. If I hadn't been there—"

"You *were* there and you're his wife now and owed all loyalty and respect," Aislinn interjected, her blue eyes flashing fire. Lisette could not help thinking of the formidable sight her sister-in-law must make with a sword in hand, which made her pray fervently to be half so bold and brave.

"Have courage, Lisette!" Aislinn added as if she'd read her thoughts. "You must believe with all your heart that what Conall vowed is true...for any doubt and fear can only destroy your chance for happiness. Will you promise me that you'll trust the honor in him?"

Lisette nodded, but that didn't appear to be enough for Aislinn, who looked at her sternly.

"You must swear it, too—as Conall swore to God above."

"*Oui*, I swear...as God is my witness."

"Good, I've hope for you both now."

Aislinn had only a moment to give her a hug before a sharp knock came at the door. Lisette glanced with her to see Sorcha standing behind a stout balding gentleman with a basket of vials slung over his arm...which reminded her of when she had first seen Conall.

He had carried such a basket, too, though he had been dressed in a friar's habit. This man wore a plain woolen tunic and looked harried, his face sweaty and flushed as if he had lunged up the tower steps.

"Is aught amiss, Tobias?" Aislinn asked him, hastening across the room.

"Aye, Lady Campbell, word has come that villagers jumped into the swollen creek tae save some children who were playing on the bank. Two men were lost and a bairn only five years old. The laird is bringing three other wee ones for me tae tend in the infirmary that were dragged from the water just in time. Is the lady's injury a serious one?"

"*Non*, not serious at all," Lisette answered before Aislinn could say a word, though her sister-in-law quickly grabbed a roll of bandages from the basket.

"I will tend to her, Tobias. Do you have liniment?"

"Aye." The healer rummaged in the basket and handed her a dark brown vial before moving to the door, clearly anxious to return to the infirmary.

"I'll follow as soon as I'm done here," Aislinn called after him, her expression somber as she turned back to Lisette.

"God help us, a terrible tragedy. Here I've been planning your marriage feast for this coming Saturday, which should be a joyous occasion—"

"Aislinn, wasna that our secret?" blurted Sorcha, who had been hovering near the door. She looked pale, Tobias's news clearly distressing her, which made Aislinn open her arms as Sorcha rushed into her embrace.

"Shh, sweeting, it's still our secret. Lisette doesn't know everything we've arranged, do you?"

Lisette shook her head, though Sorcha had begun to sob.

"Those poor bairns..."

"Aye, we've some trying days ahead, but Tobias will help them—just as Lisette needs our help now."

As if to distract the tenderhearted girl, Aislinn drew her to where Lisette still sat at the edge of the bed and pointed to her right ankle.

"I want you to open the liniment and pour some into your hands. Will you do that for me?"

Sorcha hiccoughed and nodded, and then sank to her knees as Aislinn quietly instructed her how to massage the oily liquid smelling of mint into Lisette's ankle, her touch featherlight.

"That's right, good. When you're done, I'll wrap her foot in a bandage and then we'll go downstairs and see what else needs to be done, aye?"

Again, Sorcha nodded, so focused upon their task that she had ceased to sob and glanced up with concern at Lisette.

"Am I hurting you?"

"*Non*, sweeting, you're so very kind to help me," she murmured, using the same endearment as Aislinn, which seemed to please Sorcha.

A few moments more and Lisette's ankle was securely bandaged, while a commotion carried to them from outside in the bailey. At once Sorcha jumped up and rushed to the window.

"It's Cameron and the others—Aislinn, look!"

As her sister-in-law went to join Sorcha, Lisette wished she could glance out the window, too, but she didn't dare with her ankle. In truth, it throbbed a bit from their ministrations, but the liniment did feel cooling as Sorcha cried out again.

"There's Conall, too, do you see him? Why is that lady sharing a horse with him, Aislinn? She's very pretty, and Conall is holding a little boy with black hair, though the bairn doesna look well."

"Enough, Sorcha, let's just go and see. Lisette, you'd best stay off your ankle the rest of the day or I'd ask you to join us. Don't forget what we spoke of, will you promise me?"

Lisette murmured a soft "*Oui*," even as her sister-in-law hustled Sorcha to the door, and within another moment, they were gone.

Leaving her alone.

The cacophony of horses whinnying and men shouting no match for the thundering of her heart as she rose from the bed in spite of her initial reluctance, and hobbled to the window.

Just in time to see Conall handing a boy of mayhap four years into Cameron's outstretched arms while the woman, weeping loudly, jumped down from behind Conall and ran alongside Cameron...Lisette guessed toward the infirmary.

She guessed, too, that the young woman must be the boy's mother, her long, honey-colored hair flying behind her while Conall dismounted, his expression as grim as Lisette had ever seen it.

He glanced up at the window, clearly having seen her, but then he turned away to follow after his brother —Conall running now, too.

"Oh, Conall, will the child be all right?"

Aislinn had walked up quietly behind him in the infirmary, Conall standing to one side while Tobias hovered over a cot where a little boy coughed and sputtered.

He didn't answer her because he didn't know, his gut twisting at her query.

Creek water trickled from the boy's mouth, his face as white as death as the healer rolled him onto his stomach and pounded upon his back. Conall moved closer, the rapid-fire blows making his jaw clench, but he did not question the healer's actions though Lorna began to weep even louder.

Lorna.

He had thought he would never see her again, and yet here she stood on the opposite side of the cot, her red-rimmed eyes focused upon her son.

The past four years had not been kind to her, her still-lovely face careworn, but that hadn't been his first thought when coming upon the frantic commotion by the creek.

Two men drowned and one child. Three other bairns rescued, but two not faring well. All young boys in a group that had strayed too close to the rising water and slipped upon the muddy bank. Thankfully some villagers had heard their screams and come running, but with the tragic outcome that had ensued. There had been no time to talk, only react—Lorna and her gasping child swept up by Conall onto his horse while Cameron and his men had seen to the other two boys and their desperate parents.

Now Lorna was sobbing and her son mayhap dying, though Tobias didn't look half so grim since the boy had coughed up more of the water he'd swallowed during his near drowning.

"Aye, more in his stomach than his lungs—a good thing." With great care, the healer lifted up his small charge and settled him on an opposite cot with fresh bedding, and then covered him to his chin with a blanket. "The next few hours will tell us much, lass, but I believe your son will survive."

Tobias's low pronouncement was greeted by a piercing cry of relief from Lorna, who sank beside the cot to embrace the boy. With shaking fingers, she swept the midnight hair from his pale brow, and only then did she look up to meet Conall's gaze.

"*Your* son, too, Conall. Do you not see it?"

Conall felt as if he had been struck, he was so astonished. He glanced from Lorna's face to the boy and back again, her green eyes narrowed with bitterness.

"Aye, you left me with a mewling babe after all—

though my husband agreed tae raise him as his own. Yet every day Colin looks more like you, and Hamish couldna stomach it any longer. He's as red-headed as that one there"—Lorna pointed at Aislinn—"so everyone in our village knew that Hamish hadna sired the boy. *My* boy, aye, that's how I've looked upon him until my husband demanded that I bring him tae you!"

She nearly spat out the last words and went back to caressing the boy's pale cheek, while Conall glanced behind him at Aislinn, who looked as amazed as he must still appear.

Colin.

His son.

Conall's gaze flew to Cameron, who stood near the bedside of one of the other boys, where Tobias had taken the place of an assistant trying to revive him.

Yet a moment later, a keening wail broke from the throat of a second mother who'd followed her son to the fortress, the middle-aged woman racked by grief as the healer pulled a blanket up over the boy's face.

Another bairn dead while his son lived—at least thus far. The third boy was already sitting up and watching the somber proceedings with such a look of sadness upon his face that Conall went over to his cot.

"Your friend?" he asked gently, the boy nodding as his parents, hovering nearby, came closer to comfort him.

"Aye, leave your son's bedside without even acknowledging him tae everyone here!" Lorna blurted with such outrage in her voice that several people gasped, Aislinn included. "So much for the love you professed tae me four years ago when you asked me tae be your wife. I suppose you'll not acknowledge me, either, and cast us out as soon as Colin's up and about again! What am I tae do with him then? I told you my husband doesna want him, and I've another wee bairn crying for my return!"

"*Enough*, woman!" Cameron's voice edged with anger, he glanced from Lorna to Conall as Aislinn hastened to his side. "We're lord and lady here and we know naught of you. If Conall had asked you tae be his wife, he would have told me as much, as his elder brother—"

"I did ask her and she refused me." His tone embittered, Conall met Cameron's startled gaze. "I didna tell you because there was no point tae doing so. Lorna left Argyll and went east tae Perthshire with her new husband, a blacksmith. She didna want tae wed a warrior and spurned my love when I told her I wasna free tae take up another trade—not with Earl Seoras as my overlord. Are you satisfied, Cameron? Have you heard enough?"

Conall's jaw had clenched so tight that it was hard to speak, his brother staring silently at him while Aislinn looked at him with pity.

"I didna know she bore a child...*my son*. You can see well enough that I sired him, aye? Raven-black hair and blue eyes, a Campbell through and through!"

Conall had shouted, such anger and resentment welling inside him over Lorna's long ago betrayal—and that she had never let him know about Colin—that he could but storm from the infirmary.

He needed air. He needed to clear his head! He strode back into the bailey and roared for his horse—Conall pacing in circles until a flush-faced stable boy came running with his stallion saddled and snorting as if affronted to have been pulled from his stall and fresh hay.

Conall mounted and then roared again, this time for the fortress gates to be opened for him. He veered his horse sharply around and dug in his heels, a glance at the tower nearest the keep making him swear under his breath as he rode out.

Lisette still stood there at the window as if watching

for him, waiting for him...the bright promise of the present colliding with a tortured past that he had tried so hard to forget—God help him!

He had a son!

CHAPTER 13

"I don't have much else to tell you," Aislinn murmured, squeezing Lisette's hand as they sat side by side on the edge of the bed. "Well, other than Conall's not yet returned and it's almost time for supper. I would have come sooner, but I stayed at the infirmary since someone should be with her..."

Aislinn fell silent, but Lisette could guess what she was thinking.

Conall should have remained with his young son and the child's mother, Lorna. A beautiful name for a woman Conall had loved four years ago...and lost.

So much made sense now after what Aislinn had shared with her, Lisette swallowing hard against the tightness in her throat and the tears threatening to fall.

She had seen him ride out from the fortress hours ago, leaving her in their bedchamber alone and confused as to what might have happened, so many questions running through her mind.

Who was the woman? Why had Conall gone running after her? Did he know her and the boy? Or had he simply helped out some strangers in the village and had rushed to the infirmary to see how they fared?

One look at Aislinn's somber face when she entered the room a short while ago had told Lisette that her sis-

ter-in-law had come to provide her some answers...
though she wished she had remained ignorant for the
piercing pang in her heart.

Dear God, did Conall still love Lorna? The woman he'd
asked to marry him and who had borne him a
son...Colin.

A fine name for a handsome boy, for how could he
be otherwise with Conall as his father? It was easy for
her to imagine the child's black hair and eyes as blue as
the deep ocean that she had crossed with Isabeau to
come to Scotland.

Now tears did tumble down her face, Lisette not
having thought of her half-sister for days. It wasn't even
two weeks yet since she had last seen her. Was Isabeau
content and happy with her new life? Her new husband?
So much had happened in such a short time and now
this startling news—

"Colin is doing better, heaven be praised," Aislinn
said in a hushed voice that broke into Lisette's tortured
thoughts. "The other boy that survived has already returned to the village with his parents while the one that
died—ah, God, to lose one's child. I pray that you and I
never know such grief..."

Aislinn had let go of Lisette's fingers to touch her
stomach, which made Lisette's heart seem to jump.

"Aislinn, are you with child?"

"I don't know yet...mayhap. I've not bled this
month, but it's too soon to tell—*oh!*"

Lisette had flung her arms around Aislinn to embrace her, her beautiful sister-in-law breaking into soft
laughter. Lisette laughed, too, but only for a moment
before the weight of the day's events crept back into
her mind and she released Aislinn to rise from
the bed.

She winced a little at the twinge in her ankle, but it
was nothing compared to earlier in the day. The liniment had worked wonders, which made it so much

easier to walk to the window where she'd spent hours waiting for Conall, watching for him...

"I'm sure he'll return before it grows dark," she heard Aislinn murmur, though Lisette didn't turn away from her post. "I'm sure he's wondering, too, about Colin. I've never seen him look so shocked as when Lorna blurted out that the boy was his son. Mayhap that's what so angered him...not knowing anything about the lad. Lorna plans to leave for Perthshire as soon as Colin is up and playing again. She says he's a good-natured boy in spite of her husband's dislike of him—"

"Oh, *non*, I hope he didn't beat the child!" That terrible thought had made Lisette spin from the window and meet Aislinn's eyes. "Mayhap that's why she's so eager to leave Colin here. He wasn't safe with her husband."

"All the more reason for you and Conall to make him feel as safe as possible and give him as much love as you can muster."

"Muster?"

"Aye, for another woman's child. A woman that Conall loved at one time—"

"Or mayhap loves still." That same pang assailing her, Lisette swiped away the wetness blurring her vision even as Aislinn shook her head sternly.

"Lorna's married to another man, Lisette. Even if they wanted to, she and Conall could never remain together, and there is so much anger between them—aye, even hatred on Lorna's part, though I don't fully understand why."

"Conall wouldn't change his life for her," Lisette said almost to herself, though her soft words made Aislinn nod. "She wanted him to find another trade, or so you told me that's what he said. You told me as well that love and hatred are a double-edged sword—ah, God."

Lisette turned away and leaned her forehead against

the window, despair overwhelming her even as Aislinn jumped up from the bed and rushed over to her.

"No, you mustn't think Conall will mayhap betray you! I've seen how he looks at you, remember? I didn't see him look at Lorna at all the same as he does with you—if anything only with pity, just as I felt for him to learn in so startling a manner of his son. Lorna is lovely, aye, but with a haggardness that comes when life has been hard and unkind. The marriage bed she made with her blacksmith, Hamish, must be as unhappy as the life she envisioned with Conall, a warrior sworn to serve a harsh overlord—"

"All the more reason for her not to want to leave him now, no matter what she says!" Lisette pushed away from the window and limped over to the fireplace, nothing upon the iron grate now but smoldering logs crumbling into ash.

Just as her new life with Conall felt as if it were crumbling into ash.

No wonder he had said he could not promise her love. *His heart still belonged to another*! If there was a chance that he was falling in love with her, as Aislinn had claimed just that morning, surely all of those burgeoning feelings must have vanished to see Lorna again.

His true love.

The woman he had not been able to forget in spite of his dalliances—*mon Dieu*!

All of that secret suffering and heartache and vowing never to marry had been because of Lorna!

"Lisette, you're walking well enough now," came Aislinn's voice behind her as Lisette stared unseeing into the glowing embers. "Come with me to supper."

"*Non*, I'll stay here."

Lisette heard a heavy sigh, but Aislinn did not argue with her. Instead, she clasped Lisette's fingers as if making one last attempt to reassure her and then left the room, closing the door with a low thud behind her.

It might have been the sound of Lisette's heart breaking in two as her fondest hope for a happy life with Conall faded and sputtered like a dying spark beneath the grate.

Never before had she wished she had told him at the church that she wasn't Isabeau, but Lisette did now...

~

Conall bounded up the tower steps, everything accomplished that he had set for himself except for one most important task.

He felt so much better since speaking with the priest at the village church, his heart and his step lighter. He had rode out of the fortress consumed by anger that Lorna had never let him know about his son —their son!—and he still felt a twinge of bitterness, he was human after all and no saint.

Yet the worst of that dark emotion had eased at the priest's admonishment to simply be thankful for Colin's arrival and to look to the future. Not the past. A future with a new wife and a son to protect and provide for... and mayhap an even bigger family one day if heaven blessed him and Lisette with more children.

That thought made him hasten toward their bed-chamber down a hallway lit with flickering candles in wall sconces, for the hour was late.

Before he'd made his way to the church, he had tried to clear his head with a long ride, so it had been near dusk when he finally left the priest. It was well past supper now, but there had been much to do before he would allow himself to seek out Lisette—och, he hoped she would understand that he hadn't purposely avoided her.

Aislinn had pulled him aside shortly after arriving back at the fortress to tell him that she had spoken to

Lisette about Colin...and Lorna. He hadn't been irritated by this news, given that he had ridden out in such a fury without first visiting with Lisette, which would have been the caring thing to do.

He had seen her standing in the window, no doubt with questions whirling in her mind, but he had left anyway—aye, like any man, he could be an utter fool at times. When Aislinn told him that Lisette had refused to accompany her to the great hall for the evening meal, he knew then that she must think the worst.

Of him, aye, he had no doubt. What wife wouldn't when faced with a husband's lost love and a four-year-old bairn that she must now help him to raise?

Lost love no longer. As Conall pushed open the door, he felt little emotion in thinking of Lorna, his only consideration for Lisette.

The room was dimly lit and quiet, one candle burning and no warming blaze in the fireplace, which made him wonder about the servants' inattention as his gaze flew to the bed. She must be asleep, but when he drew closer, she wasn't there—and only then did he hear the creak of a chair from a darkened corner of the room.

"Lisette?"

She didn't answer, though he could hear the softness of her breathing, which quickened his heartbeat.

It felt like days since he had last seen her when it had been mere hours, Cameron having quietly awakened him and whispered about the flooding in the village from all the rain. Conall had climbed out of bed with great reluctance, and left her only after tucking the covers snugly around her to keep her safe and warm.

Yet the air in the room had grown cool, which made him stride with a low curse to the fireplace to stack logs and restore a healthy blaze. All the while, Lisette didn't stray from the chair, though Conall could feel her gaze upon him.

Not angry or jealously upset, which wouldn't have been like her sweet temperament at all. Just a sadness emanating from her that made Conall furious with himself for not coming to her straightaway to tell her what had transpired.

After a last stoking of the fire with the poker, he turned to face her with an apology upon his lips, to find that she had risen and gone to the window.

He hadn't even heard her for her bare feet padding silently upon the floor.

Her white nightgown illuminated by the moonlight streaming into the room, her dark brown hair framing her face and flowing down her back.

His breath caught at how lovely she looked, though his gut twisted at the tears shimmering in her eyes.

"Lisette, I—"

"Is your son well, Conall?"

He nodded, moving closer, but she seemed to shrink away from him and turned her head to look outside. He could see that her chin trembled and she was trying not to weep, which made him inwardly curse himself for hurting her...however unintentionally.

"Wife, will you hear me out?" he asked gently, standing in place though he longed to reach out and take her into his arms. "I would have come tae you sooner, but I went first tae the infirmary tae see if Colin was faring better. I should never have left his side...it was callous of me and unthinking—"

"*Oui*."

Conall blinked at her soft-spoken rebuke, which was as close as she had come to indignation since the night she'd awoken from the sleeping potion. She still stared out the window, too, as if refusing to look at him. Strangely, he felt like chuckling, but that wouldn't help the situation—och, not at all.

"Colin *is* better, Lisette, so much so that Tobias agreed for me tae take him and his mother tae a comfortable room in the opposite tower. I know you havna met my son yet...or Lorna, but you would want that for them, aye? You've a kind heart...as good and kind as I've ever known. That's why I'm here with *you*—no matter what you mayhap fear will happen. Will you look at me now?"

Lisette hesitated, smudging the tears from her eyes with the palm of her hand, but to Conall's relief, she met his eyes.

He saw hurt in those luminous brown depths, yet a glimmer of hope, too, his heart thudding harder at how beautiful she looked in the soft moonlight. Aye, more stunning a woman than he deserved...while he ached even more to embrace her.

"At one time I loved Lorna, I'll not tell you anything less than the truth, and I wanted tae wed her. Yet it wasna meant tae be, do you hear me? Lorna will always be Colin's mother, but it's you that will help me tae rear him, Lisette. It's a hard thing she must do tae leave him with us, but it's for the best. She knows it and so do I. Will you show her in the morning that you'll love and care for the boy? It would give her some comfort..."

Conall fell silent, knowing the great task he was asking of Lisette even as she nodded and swiped away a fresh tear from her cheek.

"He will be as my own child—oh, Conall, so you don't still love her? If you did, I wouldn't blame you, she's so very lovely—"

"Lorna doesna love me. Nor I, her." With one step, he pulled Lisette into his arms and hugged her, relief swamping him again when she wound her arms around his waist. It felt so wondrous just to hold her that for a long moment, he simply stood there and breathed in the scent of her, his face pressed to her damp cheek.

Damp with tears he had caused, but by God, he swore he would never again subject her to such pain.

"Do you know where I was before I returned tae

the fortress?" he said against her ear. "The village church, talking with the priest. A wise man. He told me tae look ahead and not behind me. I've been so bitter these past four years, yet no one guessed it from the way I lived. When I wasna fighting, I was laughing and amusing myself—aye, frivolous dalliances, King Robert pegged me well. Everything I did was tae forget Lorna... but it's you, Lisette, who has set me free. *I love you.*"

CHAPTER 14

I f Conall had shouted, Lisette couldn't have been more stunned at his fervent declaration, and she froze in his arms.

"Y-you love me?"

"Aye, woman, mayhap from the first moment I saw you twirling in place with your eyes closed and the sweetness of your laughter filling the air. Forgive me. I've given you so little cause for happiness—"

"*Non*, Conall, you holding me brings me happiness! Your love..." Lisette found she could no longer speak for the emotion overwhelming her, her heartbeat drumming in her ears. She might have stood frozen a moment before, but now she could not hug him closely enough as he found her mouth with a kiss that stole her breath.

Tender and yet achingly fierce as if pouring out the emotion that seemed to grip him, too. He held her as fiercely, locking her within an embrace so tight that she felt the rampant beating of his heart against her breast.

She could have remained there forever, moonlight spilling around them, his kiss making her lightheaded with elation, her knees gone weak. He must have felt her falter for she was suddenly swept from her feet, Lisette gasping.

An instant later and she was lying upon the bed and staring wide-eyed at Conall, who had stepped away to hastily strip in front of her.

A sword belt thunked to the floor, followed by the heavy thud of his boots.

A breacan went flying to land upon a chair.

A tunic was hauled over his head to reveal a masculine form so powerful, so beautiful to behold, that Lisette gasped again...feeling giddy at the intensity of his eyes upon her.

Not the deep vibrant blue that could make her breath catch whenever he looked at her, but darkened in the firelight to almost black.

He stood fully naked now, his body so formidable from the breadth of his shoulders to the tapering of his hips and his thighs thick with muscle. A single stride brought him back to the bed while Lisette could but sink against the pillows and watch him in wonder.

"It's been too long, wife...*too long*."

She knew he meant the night they had consummated their marriage, but she had little time to think further upon it at all when Conall climbed onto the bed and blanketed her with his body.

The weight of him pressed her into the mattress.

The warmth of him through her nightgown made her shiver with anticipation.

She sucked in her breath and closed her eyes, awaiting his knee spreading her legs apart...only to hear a low chuckle as Conall shifted his weight and raised himself on his elbows.

"Open your eyes, sweet Lisette."

She did, giggling now, too, at the teasing smile that greeted her and made her heart leap and flutter.

She had never seen him look at her thusly, a playful side of Conall she had not known until that moment.

He looked younger to her in the firelight as if a great burden had been lifted from him, Lisette sending a prayer of thanks for the priest who had encouraged him to look to the future—*their future*! She felt as if she were witnessing another miracle as Conall chuckled even more deeply, his smile broadening, and then he rolled with her onto his back so suddenly that she cried out in surprise.

Yet an instant later and she giggled, too, his light-heartedness infectious as she gazed down at him and swept aside an unruly shock of black hair from his forehead.

"If I'd known Highlanders were so handsome, I would have prayed to come to Scotland sooner."

"*Highlanders?*" he teased back, the husky rumble of his voice giving her shivers. "Or one Highlander..."

"Ah, Conall...only one. You." Lisette had sobered just as he had, his gaze grown serious as he reached up to twirl a lock of her hair around his finger.

"I dinna wish tae press you, lass...but do you think mayhap one day you might love me, too?"

Lisette stilled atop him, so dumbstruck that she didn't answer, her heart stuck in her throat.

Did he not know? Could he not see? Conall had sounded so hopeful and even uncertain of what she might say, which made her stare at him in utter astonishment.

"Och, forgive me for asking—it was foolish of me. Of course it will take you some time. We've known each other for no more than two weeks, though I would swear from how you look at me..."

He fell silent, cradling her face now with a hand that felt callused and rough. A strong hand that had wielded a sword in countless battles, only to touch her now with such tenderness, Lisette felt tears well in her eyes.

"Oh, Conall, I—"

She wasn't able to finish for he had raised himself up to kiss her, both hands holding her face as his mouth plundered hers.

She sensed a turbulence in him now and wondered if she'd hurt him not to answer him more readily, but a ripping sound made her forget all else when he tore her nightgown from her body.

Conall still kissing her as he drew her down atop him, his tongue demanding entrance, her bare breasts pressed into the hardness of his chest.

The tenderness she had felt had fled and in its place, a man ravenous to possess her, his kiss only deepening with a wildness that filled her with sudden anguish.

Ah, God, she had hurt him! She tried to pull away to finish what she had meant to say, but he held her so tightly, his arms steely around her while his kiss grew more impassioned.

Lisette could do naught else but surrender to him and return his kiss with equal fervor, which made him groan against her mouth.

Later she would tell him how much she loved him, but for now...

Lisette gasped, all thought fleeing as his hand slipped beneath their bodies to tease the spot already slick and yearning for him.

It had been too long—*too long* for her, too!

She gasped again when his fingers retreated and he lifted her hips with both hands to guide her down upon him, Conall thrusting upward with the hardness of his body.

Filling her with the length of him, the thickness of him, while Lisette trembled from head to foot, moaning against his mouth.

He had not for one instant ceased to kiss her, his tongue spearing into her even as his thrusts quickened and deepened...until his body grew stiff beneath her and a ragged groan burst from his throat.

Her own outcry echoed his release, Lisette so blinded by the ecstasy that shook her, she could but collapse upon him dizzying moments later.

Breathless.

Her fingers tunneled into the sweat-damped hair upon his chest.

The strong thud of his heartbeat against her ear.

Their bodies still joined and a warm wetness slicking her inner thighs from the seed that he'd spilled inside her.

She couldn't move and she didn't try to...Conall still embracing her though she felt him relax beneath her, his breathing gradually becoming slow and sated.

She heard a low rumble from his chest and knew he had succumbed to sleep, the tumult of the day catching up with him even as her own eyelids drifted closed.

She kissed him then...where his steady heartbeat lulled her, Lisette's fervent whisper to him slowly fading.

"*Je t'aime*, Conall...*je t'aime*."

~

"I hate you, Euan MacCulloch...*hate you*."

Hissing under her breath, Isabeau tried to shift her naked body away from her husband's, but there was no use. In sleep, his arm lay heavily upon her like a dead weight—*mon Dieu*, how she wished he was dead and she was free of him!

Her jewels retrieved and mayhap Lisette dead, too, for all the trouble her bastard half-sister had cost her. If only the right time had presented itself already, each passing day to Isabeau a mounting torment.

Each passing hour, she amended, feeling nothing but disgust that Euan had rutted upon her again.

She had always thought she would enjoy lovemaking after learning to pleasure herself long before she was wed, the shivering sensations, the delicious climaxes, but her husband's constant demands upon her now only turned her stomach.

Five or six times a day, she was sickened by it! She could still hear the coarse snickering of his men outside the tent that served as her and Euan's private quarters aboard ship, their forty-oar vessel anchored in a secluded cove.

She supposed that she should be grateful to him for allowing her to accompany him north to Argyll—but it hadn't been due to anything she had said to convince him. He didn't trust her any more than she trusted him, yet mayhap it was more that he enjoyed his lustful dominance over her far too much to have left her behind in Dumfries.

"Disgusting lout," Isabeau grated to herself, relieved at least that Euan's arm had fallen away from her when he rolled onto his back and began to snore.

Right then and there she wanted to press a pillow to his face with all the strength she possessed and have done with him, not just to silence the repulsive noises coming out of his mouth. Regrettably, it wasn't time to rid herself of her husband, but she would—*oui, she had vowed it*!

A trio of spies paid by Euan had infiltrated Campbell Castle where they knew Lisette had been taken after her marriage, and the burgundy cloak was with her, too. One of them, a stout middle-aged woman working as a maidservant, had seen the garment hanging in the armoire, but there had been no opportunity for her to grab it and make her way out of the fortress.

At least that was the latest news they had received this morning from a MacDougall clansman who had spoken to another of Euan's spies, a farmer from the village who was free to move his wagon in and out of Campbell Castle with produce for the kitchen.

Lisette had reportedly been bound to her bedchamber with Lady Aislinn Campbell forever hovering around her, thwarting any attempt thus far to be done with retrieving the cloak and on their way back to Dumfries.

At any time, their ship might be discovered by those loyal to King Robert, and they would be forced to find another place to conceal their presence that wasn't as close to the fortress. So far they had been lucky with other MacDougalls supplying them with food and horses when needed, the exiled clan only too eager to lend a hand against their powerful enemies that now controlled much of Argyll.

Euan had told her what happened to Earl Seoras MacDougall in June, his head severed with one sword blow from his body by the renowned warrior Gabriel MacLachlan, who now bore the title of earl.

True, Seoras had overstepped his bounds by ruthlessly seeking the title of King of Scots for himself, and he was known for his savage cruelty that had many wishing him dead. MacLachlan and two of his captains, Cameron and Conall Campbell, had helped to save King Robert's life that day, with Cameron now a baron and laird of Campbell Castle.

It might have been Isabeau to become the wife of Conall, the younger brother, if he had arrived a few moments earlier at the convent and abducted *her* instead of Lisette. Right now, Isabeau was certain that she might have enjoyed such a fate, a sideways glance at her sleeping husband with drool dripping from his mouth making her want to reach again for a pillow.

Instead Conall, named a baron, too, and rewarded with his own castle and lands further to the north, had wed Lisette! Her station in life had risen overnight from a lowly lady's maid destined to wed one of Euan's men to another Lady Campbell, which sickened Isabeau all the more.

"Damn you, Lisette," she said through gritted teeth. She shifted further away from Euan, and yanked a blanket over her breasts as queasiness assailed her from the ship's incessant rocking.

All of this misery she blamed on her half-sister! Isabeau had thought from how swiftly they had sailed north, instead of traveling overland by horseback, that this entire debacle would be over and done as swiftly. Her burning hope now was that Lisette would be well enough to leave her bedchamber for a wedding feast in three days, so their spies could grab that wretched cloak and transport it to the ship, the thing done.

All that would be left to Isabeau then was devising a way to rid herself of Euan, which would leave her a wealthy widow with lands in both France and Scotland and the freedom to choose her own lovers...for she would never again marry.

Never!

CHAPTER 15

"**C**ome, I'm eager for you tae meet my son."
Lisette nodded as Conall led her by the hand toward a room where the door was ajar, the cloak he had grabbed from the armoire to wrap her in, swishing around her legs.

Isabeau's wedding cloak, though Lisette didn't mind, more grateful for its warmth than that it had once belonged to her half-sister.

The air in the fortress had grown chilly after the recent storm, the day having dawned gray and cold. It had been so hard to leave the snug comfort of their bed and she had attempted to protest. Conall had silenced her with a fervent kiss and a good squeeze to her bare rump before throwing back the covers and pulling her up with him.

Her flesh at once covered with goosebumps and her nipples puckered from the cool air, which had made Conall stare at her in so hungry a manner that she'd wondered if he might pick her up and toss her right back on the bed.

His male flesh grown thick and hard and standing at attention, which had made her giggle and marvel, too, that he could appear eager for more lovemaking when they had satisfied each other so wondrously upon first awaking.

Even now, Lisette felt her cheeks burn at the startling image in her mind of Conall lowering his head between her thighs to pleasure her with his tongue in so delirious a fashion, she felt her knees weaken at the remembering.

"Och, woman, I know what you're thinking," he whispered against her ear, letting go of her hand to wind his arm around her waist and pull her close for a kiss. Yet so brief a one that she yearned for more even as Conall looked at her with mock sternness. "Later, my love...later. Listen! I can hear Colin laughing. I had his and Lorna's belongings brought from the village, including his toys."

Indeed, the boy's playful outburst carried to them from the open door, a very good sign for his recovery that made Conall smile broadly and once again take Lisette's hand. She smiled, too, at how boyish he looked in that moment—making her heart jump and eagerness filling her to see more of this side of her husband.

The scowling Highlander she'd known during their journey north had all but disappeared, and she didn't miss him even a little. She did slow her step, though, but not because of her ankle that hardly hurt anymore. Her smile faded at her sudden nervousness.

"You mustna worry about Lorna," Conall murmured, pulling her close again for one more quick embrace. "We spoke last night when I brought her and Colin tae this room and she's eager tae meet you as well."

Warmed that Conall had sensed her unease and sought to reassure her, Lisette nonetheless didn't feel as convinced as he appeared.

She felt his fingers tighten a bit around hers, which made her certain now that he wasn't entirely sure, either, about Lorna's reception. Lisette caught her breath as he opened the door wider so they could enter, Colin's laughter ceasing as she and Conall entered the room.

The little boy—the very image of his father with his midnight hair and deep blue eyes—skittered back to his mother from where he'd been playing by the window and gazed out at them from behind her skirt. Lorna stood slightly taller than Lisette and wore a simple brown tunic belted at the waist, which accentuated the curves of her body, her honey-gold hair freshly brushed and falling to her narrow waist. It was she that laughed now, a light brittle sound, as she took his arm and pulled him around in front of her.

Not gently as Lisette might have expected, but with a sharp jerk that made Colin gasp and look up at his mother while Conall's grip on Lisette's fingers grew tighter. He hadn't released her hand, but drew her further into the room, a tenseness in him now that belied the forced smile on his face.

"Lorna...Colin...this is Lisette, my wife."

Nothing was said for what seemed the longest moment, Colin looking uncertainly from Lorna and then to Lisette before he gazed up at his father.

Way up...for Conall towered above the boy, though Colin didn't look frightened at all, just curious. His eyes wide and his mouth rounded in awe as his gaze fell to the sword at Conall's belt, and he pointed with one finger.

"May I see, Papa?"

At once Lisette felt some of the tension ease from Conall as if he had softened inside at the inquisitive request from his son, and he let go of her hand to gesture for the boy to come closer. Then he knelt down on one knee so as not to appear imposing, Colin approaching him not with any trepidation but great eagerness to touch the polished hilt.

The boy's awestruck intake of breath grew to a childish gasp as Conall slowly withdrew a third of the weapon from its sheath, but no more, as if not wanting to risk his son harming himself somehow on the blade. Only then did Lisette look up from the touching scene to see Lorna not looking at Conall and Colin—but at her.

Lorna's green eyes glittering with a coldness that pierced Lisette to the bone...no more welcome on the young woman's face than if she stared at a hated enemy.

Such dismay overcame Lisette that it was all she could do not to flee from the room, but Conall's low-spoken discourse with his son made her stay rooted in place.

"One day you will wield such a sword, Colin. Would that please you?"

"Oh, aye, Papa! Will I grow tall and strong like you and have a sword as big?"

Conall's chuckling warmed Lisette's heart even as Lorna's relentless glare chilled her, and his nod made Colin clap his small hands together and hop up and down with excitement.

In truth, Lisette was amazed that the child so readily called Conall "Papa," but clearly Lorna had prepared the boy for the new life he would know as a Campbell. Lisette's mouth dropped open in surprise when Colin suddenly reached out for her hand, though he glanced behind him at Lorna before taking her fingers.

"Aye, Colin, Lady Campbell will be your new mother after I return home tae Hamish and your little sister—"

"Oh, Mama, will I see you again?"

Colin's plaintive query stilling Lisette's breath, she saw only that Lorna's expression had hardened into something not beautiful at all but as harsh as her tone.

"Mayhap if your father grants us a visit—but

enough, Colin! Go back tae your blocks by the window."

Obediently, the boy obliged her, though he looked over his small shoulder as Conall rose to his feet.

"Of course you may visit, Lorna, I've already told you as much," he said tersely, once again reaching for Lisette's hand.

Gratefully, she took it, the warm strength of his fingers soothing away some of the chill that had not left her. She saw that Lorna had noted their joined hands with an impassive expression, yet it was the open jealousy in those emerald depths that reflected exactly how she felt as she looked from Conall back to her.

"Mayhap, but I'm sure your bonny bride would prefer that we go our separate ways, aye, *Lisette?*"

She blanched, Lorna's hostile tone so reminiscent of Isabeau's that she faltered now and looked uncertainly at Conall.

"I...I think I should go. I'm sure you and Lorna have more to discuss—"

"Nothing that's not tae be said in front of you, wife."

His voice brusque and stern, all good humor fled from his darkened expression, Lisette could only nod at him as he addressed Lorna.

"I had thought you might wish tae accompany us tae our new home so you can see where Colin will live—but clearly your suggestion tae go our separate ways is the better plan. You've some of Hamish's kinsmen awaiting you in the village, aye?"

Lorna nodded stiffly. "Four of his cousins that escorted us tae Campbell Castle."

"Good, and I'll provide six of my own men tae see you safely home. The roads will be muddy and treacherous for a few days after the rain, so you'll stay here with Colin for a short while longer. I'll not have your husband saying I didna do my part tae protect you while you're in Argyll. You're welcome tae invite your kinsmen tae our wedding feast if you wish."

"I willna attend and neither will Hamish's cousins... no offense intended. I've nothing fine tae wear and they're of common stock like my husband. I doubt they would be comfortable in such grand company—"

"F-forgive me, Lorna," Lisette broke in softly, grateful for having found a way to mayhap reach out to her. "I've gowns newly made and I'm sure one would fit you—and if not, I'll have a seamstress alter it for you... and make some new clothes for Colin as well. You can choose whichever one you like—"

"Aye, a kind and generous offer from my wife and one I hope you'll accept," Conall interjected, giving Lisette's hand a gentle squeeze. "We would be pleased if you attend the feast with Colin...mayhap your last night together for a time. We know leaving him with us canna be easy for you."

"*Truly?*" Lorna had drawn herself up and lifted her chin, her eyes welling as she fixed her gaze upon Lisette. "May you never know the sorrow of giving up a child, Lady Campbell, and may you never hear your husband make such a demand of you—*any* dreadful demand. You may think Conall an honorable man, but I knew him when he promised me the moon and stars! Yet in the end, he would not trade his station as a warrior for another that would keep him safe with me, so I lied and told him I didna love him and made light of our time together."

"Lorna, *stop*—"

"No, Conall, you will hear it! Distraught from your betrayal, I married Hamish in a wild rush and the thing was done, no going back! Then I bore your son, your *bastard* bairn, and life grew harsher still. Hamish tolerated him, but he hated the boy"—Lorna lowered her voice to a hiss—"and sometimes I detested the lad, too, for every moment that he reminded me of you. Love and hate for a sweet innocent child who I'll soon leave behind me—och, Conall, look at the wretch I've become for having once loved you!"

Her pained outcry making Colin cease playing to rush to his mother and throw his arms around her knees, Lisette felt certain from the furious look upon Conall's face that he would wrest the boy from her.

Lorna loved Colin and yet hated him? Even so, such pity welled inside her for the woman, that she grabbed Conall's arm to stay him, soft pleading in her voice.

"Please, let's leave them for now. It's so difficult a time for Lorna and Colin—*please*, Conall. Later when your anger has cooled, you can talk again and mayhap decide what else to do. I don't believe for a moment that Colin is in danger here—*oui*, Lorna? Give them these last days together..."

Lorna nodded desperately as if realizing what she had revealed, while Conall swore under his breath and turned on his heel to leave Lisette staring after him.

"You see?" came Lorna's hoarse query as Conall stormed from the room. "He didna heed you at all! You think you know the man you've married—but you dinna know him! How can you after so short a time? Aislinn told me in the infirmary how you came tae be wed only days ago. I knew him for weeks longer and look what he did tae me! I tasted his love just like you—aye, run after him, Lady Campbell, and see how long you'll hold him!"

Lisette did, hastening to the door with Lorna's words ringing in her ears.

Her heart pounding.

Her stomach still churning from hearing Lorna calling her son a bastard.

Bastard! How many times had Isabeau railed at her so cruelly and called her the same?

By the time she was out in the hall, Conall had disappeared down the steps and she could but follow after him, the joy of the morning fled.

Yet what had she expected? Lorna would welcome her with open arms? Conall had seemed so sure that all would be well, yet it wasn't well.

A woman who hated her—hated Conall—slamming the door so fiercely behind her that Lisette jumped.

She could hear Colin sobbing from inside the room and she turned around, wondering if she had been wrong and mayhap the boy was in danger.

Would Lorna truly harm him?

Did she despise Conall so much that she would tease him with the prospect of rearing his son and then do something even more reckless than marrying her blacksmith years ago? Something akin to revenge that would take Colin from him forever?

As if Conall shared her thoughts, he came bounding up the steps and she hastened toward him, two somber-faced guards hard upon his heels. Within three strides, he met her and pushed her firmly against the wall.

"Dinna move, Lisette."

His voice sounded so harsh, his eyes darkened with anger, and he gestured for the guards to follow him to Lorna's room where he shoved open the door.

Lisette heard her anguished cry and Colin's heightened sobs, and then Conall rushed out with the weeping boy though Colin had flung his little arms around his father's neck.

Another moment and they had reached Lisette while the two guards barricaded the hastily shut door with their bodies—Lorna banging upon it and calling out for her son.

Her cries desperate and heartrending, which made Lisette's eyes blur with tears even as Conall, supporting Colin with one arm, took her by the hand and drew her along with him.

If he had seemed furious moments before, now he looked grimly resolute as they went down the steps together.

Colin hiccoughing and murmuring brokenly, "Mama...M-mama."

CHAPTER 16

"Colin seems happier now," Conall murmured to Lisette, who stood next to him watching his son at play in his new surroundings with Sorcha giggling at his side.

The two bairns, one only four years old and the other thirteen, might have made an incongruous pair due to the difference in their ages—but from their laughter, Conall knew he had made the right choice to bring them together.

As soon as Sorcha had entered Colin's room down the hall from Conall and Lisette's own bedchamber, the boy had ceased his muted sobbing and smiled again. Aye, thank God for the resilience of children!

Sorcha had suffered greatly for one so young and Conall suspected his son had suffered, too, during his short life—och, he could hardly bear to think of it. Yet Colin had a stalwartness to him that made relief melded with pride swell inside Conall, his newly attained role of fatherhood awaking emotions within him that he'd never before experienced.

Just as his beautiful Lisette with her arm laced through his own made him feel as if life had become complete in a way that he could never have imagined. He had been blessed with a wife and a son almost

149

overnight...the depth of the protectiveness he felt for them like nothing he had ever known, either.

Aye, he and Cameron had always been protective of each other, the two of them surviving many a bloody skirmish by watching each other's backs. Yet for the woman he loved and his boy—och, if anyone came close to causing them harm, as Lorna had done hours ago with Colin, his response would be swift and fierce.

He had shoved in that door just in time, Lorna's hand raised to strike Colin a second blow, his cheek reddened already by a slap to the face. That she would take out her jealousy and anger upon an innocent child filled Conall with disgust, and made him all the more relieved to see Colin laughing and playing.

Conall believed his son had cried so inconsolably more out of confusion than anything else, the mother he loved turning upon him. Blast and damn, how many times had it happened before Lorna had brought Colin to Argyll?

"Conall?" Her fair brow furrowed with concern, Lisette looked up at him as if she had sensed his turmoil.

He hadn't told her yet of the wretched scene that had greeted him after he'd left her standing wide-eyed in the hall, not wanting her to go near Lorna again. If he hadn't needed to quickly fetch the guards, he would never have abandoned her to whatever other resentments Lorna might have spewed at her.

"I hope you dinna think me cruel for taking Colin from his mother," he murmured so Sorcha and Colin wouldn't hear him. "I had my reasons—"

"*Oui*, I saw the red mark on his cheek." Lisette squeezed his arm and looked back to where fresh giggling erupted. She smiled, but sadly, shaking her head. "Who could harm such a sweet boy? Look at him, Conall. So happy now...yet what's to happen to Lorna?"

The tremor in Lisette's voice touched Conall that

she would harbor sympathy for a woman who had shown nothing but contempt for her, which made him bend down to kiss the softness of her cheek.

"You amaze me, wife...your kindness. I want her tae be gone by morning, but what would you have me do?"

Conall knew as soon as Lisette turned her brown eyes upon him that Lorna leaving tomorrow wasn't what she had in mind.

"Give her those few more days to spend with him—but never alone, Conall. Your son has two nursemaids now to watch over him, Aislinn has seen to that, and I doubt Sorcha will ever be far from his side. You've guards posted outside the door, too, and more guards to watch Lorna, so he'll be more than safe. She must love him deeply to have wept so when you brought him near-drowned to the fortress."

"Aye, I saw you watching from the window and wondered what you must be thinking." Conall sighed heavily, unsure of Lisette's request even as he wanted to please her and have her know that her view mattered to him. She had been so quiet these past few hours, which made him certain that something was troubling her. "I dinna know what Lorna said tae you, but I pray you dinna take it tae heart. I couldna leave my sworn post as warrior tae Earl Seoras even if I'd begged him. Here all this time I believed she betrayed me, making me act a careless fool for years when all the while, she blamed me for betraying her—och, who can make sense of such things?"

Lisette looked at him as if astonished by his outpouring, but she had no chance to say a word when Colin came running toward them.

To Conall's surprise, the boy went straight to Lisette, his arms outstretched, and she caught him up and gave him the warmest hug.

Her smile radiant, her eyes luminous with unshed

tears as if his son had given her the greatest gift she could have imagined.

Sorcha came running to join them, too, much to Colin's delight, which made Conall's heart even more full as he imagined the joy of him and Lisette having children together...aye, lots of bairns to fill a castle and make laughter ring from the halls.

For a man who had imagined no more an existence for himself than battles and blood and meaningless liaisons, he felt as if a miracle had touched him.

The same miracle that Lisette had spoken of to King Robert while Conall had cursed the day that a bride had been foisted upon him. He could not believe it had been so short a time ago when now, he could not imagine life without her.

He yearned for only one thing more...to hear Lisette say that she loved him. He could have sworn she spoke to him when he had surrendered to exhaustion the night before, yet her words had made little sense to him. Mayhap he had simply dreamed her pressing a kiss to his chest and whispering to him—

"*Laird Campbell!*"

Conall wheeled around to find Cameron's steward, Fergus, leaning upon the doorjamb, the man's pocked face flushed from hurrying.

With a glance at Lisette, who at once hustled the startled children deeper into the room, Conall followed the winded steward into the hall where the two newly posted guards looked alarmed.

"What is it, man?"

"Y-your brother sent me tae fetch you! I dinna fully know what is amiss, but he's called for his captains and warriors tae assemble in the great hall. An urgent message arrived from Earl MacLachlan—"

"Then it can only be grim news," Conall cut him off, looking at Lisette. She stared at him wide-eyed, while Sorcha had already diverted Colin with a wooden horse that she pretended to gallop through the air.

"Go, husband," Lisette murmured, straightening her shoulders as if summoning her courage. "I'll stay here with the children—but mayhap send Aislinn to tell me what has happened if you cannot return..."

Her voice had faltered, Conall longing to embrace her but heeding instead, his duty to his brother. "Protect them with your lives," he ordered the guards, and then he was running down the hall, Fergus wheezing behind him.

Yet Conall lost the steward altogether as he sprinted down the tower steps and toward the great hall, which resounded with commotion and the aggravated shouting of Cameron's men.

A wild tumult he recognized at once as warriors stoking themselves for battle, the hair rising on the back of Conall's neck.

His blood ran faster and hotter even though he still did not know the reason for Cameron's summons, his hand fisted upon the hilt of his sword. His brother stood tall and commanding in front of the massive fireplace at the center of the hall, while a path opened for Conall through the gathered throng.

A moment more and Conall had reached Cameron, who stepped forward to meet him.

"Gabriel has sent word that the MacDougalls are reorganizing themselves tae fight against us. We've stayed within these walls for too long! We'll follow the plan he's made for his own lands, half of us remaining tae protect the fortress while the rest will ride out each day and patrol the countryside. Our strength and might must be displayed for all tae see—and you, Conall, must leave today with your warriors and family tae your lands and castle tae the north. King Robert tasked us with preventing Clan MacDougall from regaining power and by God, we willna fail him!"

"Aye, we willna fail him," Conall echoed grimly, but already Cameron had turned back to his men—with Conall's among them, he saw now as warrior after warrior gave him a nod of allegiance.

After nearly a week spent in tireless training at Campbell Castle, his men, combined with the warriors King Robert had sent with him, were as cohesive a force as he could have hoped for. All of them ready and primed for battle from the deafening roars that split the air.

Wearing armor and bristling with weapons, they would make a mighty presence indeed to any that might be thinking of revolting against King Robert's rule in Argyllshire...yet Lisette and Colin would be accompanying them. Thankfully his castle lay no more than two hours' ride from the fortress, but the journey would be a dangerous one—

"Lisette is a warrior's wife—a baron's wife!" Cameron shouted at him above the uproar as if discerning Conall's thoughts. "She'll see now the responsibility that title entails, but dinna doubt her courage, brother. She's displayed enough of it since you snatched her from Dumfries, aye?"

Conall nodded as Cameron gestured for his captains to clear the great hall, though the men exiting did not cease their shouts and clamoring for battle.

His ears rang from all the noise, and he could imagine what Lisette must be thinking to hear such commotion carrying up to the tower. Lorna, too, no doubt pacing and raging in an opposite tower—Conall scowling at the thought of her. By God, what was to be done with her now?

"Lorna..." he began, but Cameron waved him to silence.

"You dinna need tae concern yourself with the woman. I've ordered five of my men tae accompany her tae the border of Perthshire but no further, for I need them here. Her kinsmen will bear the task of returning her the rest of the way tae her husband. If you wish tae bid her goodbye, you'd best hurry. They're soon tae ride out...and you're welcome, brother."

Cameron slapped him on the back and made to leave him, but Aislinn rushing forward from the direction of the kitchen made Cameron pause to sweep her into his arms. Only after a bracing kiss did he release her to stride after his men, Aislinn's lovely face flushed as red as her hair as she glanced at Conall.

"I'm so sorry, brother, but there's no time for a wedding feast now. It was to be a surprise for you and Lisette with Gabriel and Magdalene planning to attend —ah, God! Those accursed MacDougalls must be mad to think of rising up against the MacLachlans and Campbells."

In spite of the gravity facing them, Conall couldn't help smiling that Aislinn appeared ready to do battle, too, and would have pulled out a sword to emphasize her words if she'd had one strapped around her waist. After what Earl Seoras MacDougall had done to her, throwing her and her ill-fated companions into a dank hole beneath a prison cell to rot—och, but Seoras had earned his just reward and rotted himself now, in hell!

"Aislinn, will you go tae Lisette and tell her we must leave at once for our new home?"

"Aye, we've much to do. I've already ordered wagons filled with the provisions that would have been prepared for the feast and several servants have stepped forward to accompany you, along with one of the nursemaids. They'll help Lisette to get everything running smoothly. A young priest as well only just arrived at Campbell Castle. We already have Father Simeon to minister to us, so we don't need two of them."

"A priest?" Conall queried, but then he shrugged, imagining that the castle King Robert had granted him had its own chapel in want of cleric. "I must go. Cameron told me that Lorna is soon tae leave—"

"Good riddance, too, the harpy! You may have cared for her once, Conall, but you've been graced with a true gift from heaven in Lisette. Have you told her yet that you love her? Cameron and I have seen it as plain as daylight upon your face and I was almost ready to kick you to get you to see it—"

"Aye, sister, she knows it well." Conall gave Aislinn a quick embrace and then took off after Cameron before she could berate him any further, however fondly.

As soon as he stepped outside, the day still gray with heavy clouds portending more rain, he grew tense at the look Lorna gave him from where she stood ready to mount a dappled mare.

Her green eyes filled with bitterness and her chin tilted defiantly.

Conall didn't wish to linger over any goodbye, just to thank her for bringing him Colin. As soon as he drew closer, Lorna rushed toward him to his surprise and threw her arms around his neck to plant a fervent kiss upon his lips.

He stepped back at once to disengage himself from her, but still she clung to him, threading her fingers in his hair.

"My parting gift tae you, Conall Campbell...the seeds of doubt well planted."

She glanced upward then, laughing as he followed her gaze to the tower window where Lisette stood holding Colin in her arms.

Her face pale and stricken, while Sorcha appeared beside her to take the sobbing boy and then recede from view. Lisette remained there...staring at him, until a moment later she left the window, too.

"Damn you, woman—*damn you*!" Conall didn't care that he was rough with Lorna as he pulled her by the arm to her horse and lifted her into the saddle.

She laughed still, a cold, brittle sound, but when he thrust the reins into her hands and squeezed her fingers, fiercely, she gasped in pain.

"You brought me my son, Lorna, but hear this now. You willna see Colin again until he's grown into a man and will decide for himself if you're worthy of his acquaintance. He will know that Lisette showed you kindness and wished for you tae stay so you might have more time with him, but you dinna deserve such compassion even if circumstances hadna changed. Now go!"

Conall slapped the mare's rear before Lorna could retort. The horse's lunge forward made her shriek and struggle to regain control as Cameron's men closed in around her and rode with her from the bailey.

Conall did not wish her harm, but at that moment, if Lorna had fallen and broken her neck, he wouldn't have blinked an eye.

He glanced at the tower again where he had seen Lisette, but the window was still empty.

Cursing under his breath, Conall knew there was no time to go to her.

He turned from the keep and strode away to organize his men, the noise and commotion building around him.

CHAPTER 17

"**Y**ou've a fine warm cloak, Lady Campbell—a good thing now that we're closer tae the sea and with the wind picking up."

Lisette heaved a small sigh at Father Philip once again drawing his horse near to her own mount to converse with her, the young man more gregarious than any priest she'd ever known. Yet mayhap it was because he looked no more than a youth with his smooth face and pale blue eyes, his duties as a cleric of listening daylong to penitents' transgressions not yet weighing upon him.

She murmured a soft "*Oui*," but truly that was all she could muster. She gazed ahead to where Conall rode at the front of a long column of warriors, some marching while others rode two by two. Behind her rumbled a half dozen wagons and then more warriors armed to the teeth with weapons.

Swords and knives and spears and wicked-looking axes, as if they marched straight toward battle, which made her shiver though not from lack of warmth.

Aislinn had told her of the MacDougall clan's folly —for what else could it be than foolhardiness with such an impressive force to reckon with if they dared to attack? Cameron and a host of his warriors had accompanied them for a good distance and then had veered off to ride back through the countryside, their whoops and bloodcurdling bellowing enough to discourage any enemies that might be lurking along the way.

Conall's men, though, were silent and ever watchful, Conall turning every now and then to look in her direction though mayhap he was simply checking the progress of their cavalcade.

He did so now, which made Lisette's cheeks grow hot at the somber look he gave her, but then he turned around in the saddle, his back stiff and straight. She doubted that she had ever seen him appear more fearsome with his thick leather armor and a chain mail coif that covered his head and shoulders. Many of his men wore the same battle garb, which only heightened the air of danger surrounding them.

She could sense the tension emanating from him that all of his warriors seemed to share from their grim faces, while in the wagon directly behind her slept Colin in his nursemaid's arms as if he didn't know a care in the world.

His sobbing at the tower window had ceased almost as soon as Sorcha had taken him from her, which had been a good thing because Lisette had lost all strength to hold him.

Such a terrible pang struck her again at the image in her mind of Lorna rushing into Conall's embrace, the two of them kissing. *Mon Dieu*, would she ever be free of the wretched memory?

Everything afterward had happened in a blur...Aislinn rushing into the room to share what had happened and helping to pack. Then the sorrowful goodbyes to her and Sorcha while Conall had come near only once to bring a gentle brown mare for Lisette to ride instead of joining Colin and his nursemaid and the servants in the wagon. Conall had helped her to mount, his strong hands lifting her with ease, but he had said nothing, as if focused upon the perilous journey that lay ahead of them.

Oddly enough, Father Philip had his own horse, an older gelding that still plodded beside her horse though Lisette kept her eyes forward so as not to encourage the priest in further discourse. She felt too heartsick to say another word. Her gaze once again flew to Conall, who had looked behind him again and gestured toward something in the distance.

Had he done so to her or to all of them? Lisette guessed the latter when the warriors around her began to pick up their pace, and the creaking wagons, too.

She saw it then as her mare trotted past a copse of trees. A great edifice of stone rising from a promontory that jutted out over the sea, which appeared a vast expanse as gray as the overcast sky.

A second Campbell Castle...her new home. If not for what she had seen in the bailey earlier that afternoon when Lorna pressed her lips to Conall's, Lisette might have felt great excitement and joy. Instead, sadness and disbelief rippled through her as fresh as when she had stood in shock at the window.

To think the woman would be visiting her son at this place for years to come after what she had done, kissing Conall for all to see.

For Lisette to see, too. Lorna had glanced up and spied her before Conall had strode out into the bailey, and cast her a smug smile as if to remind Lisette of what she'd claimed earlier.

You think you know the man you've married—but you dinna know him!

Not for the first time, Lisette berated herself for deceiving Conall into a marriage he hadn't wanted. He had said that he thought her kind and good, but how could she be? She had lied to him and brought this misery down upon herself!

Of course a man who had known such a free existence would not be content with one woman to love for his lifetime...if he even loved her. They had known each other only days after all, just as Lorna had said.

I knew him for weeks longer and look what he did tae me!

The shrill words echoed in Lisette's mind as the wind buffeted her...smelling of the sea and whipping up white-capped waves that crashed against the rocks at the base of the promontory.

Now her teeth chattered and she drew the cloak closer around her, then glanced behind her to see that the nursemaid had thankfully bundled Colin into a blanket.

The little boy had awoken and stared around him, a sweet smile lighting his face when he spied Lisette. She smiled back, though her heart was breaking—Colin's blue eyes so like his father's.

His smile so like his father's, too, though she had glimpsed it so rarely from Conall. She thought of the night before when he had been so boyish and playful, not long after he had said he loved her.

He had said, too, that everything he'd done had been to forget Lorna—but clearly, for her to kiss him so passionately, they must still mean something to each other, Lisette was certain of it. How was she to bear it? What was she to do?

Lisette blinked away the unshed tears clinging to her lashes as another vivid memory came to her that seemed to refute her heartache, Aislinn's fervent plea echoed in her mind.

You must believe with all your heart that what Conall vowed is true...for any doubt and fear can only destroy your chance for happiness. Will you promise me that you'll trust the honor in him?

Conall had sworn to Aislinn that his wanton days were behind him, as God was his witness!

Lisette had sworn, too, as God was *her* witness, making a promise to Aislinn that she had forgotten altogether at the sight of Lorna tunneling her fingers in Conall's midnight hair and his arms around her—

"You look troubled, Lady Campbell," came Father Philip's voice to tear her from her roiling thoughts, but Lisette shook her head.

"*Non*, I'm fine, truly," she murmured, but she wasn't fine! Again she had lied, and this time to a priest whom she imagined only wished to help her.

Yet what did Father Philip know of the awful torment she would face with a husband who mayhap had no intention of remaining true to her and their marriage? What did that other priest know who had counseled Conall at the village church to look ahead and not behind him? *They* were not the ones tempted with honeyed hair and flashing green eyes and a lush body that Conall had held so close to him!

Her stomach pitching at the image she could not banish from her mind, Lisette had all she could do to keep her hands firmly upon the reins with fingers that felt ice-cold.

Their entourage had drawn closer to the castle...so close now that she could see men lining the battlements, a great shout going up among them to open the immense gates.

She imagined they must be some of Gabriel Mac-Lachlan's warriors sent to keep the fortress secure until Conall's arrival, since Gabriel was earl and ranked above Conall and Cameron, as barons. What would they find once inside those high walls? A keep and other buildings still ravaged by battle? Aislinn had told her that this castle had also belonged to the MacDougalls, but King Robert was determined to fully oust the once powerful clan from Argyll no matter how long it might take him.

Lisette sighed, thinking of the work that no doubt lay ahead of her to set the household to rights, a daunting task for any new lady of the castle.

Yet Colin's laughter distracted her and she twisted around to see the nursemaid struggling with the boy to keep him well covered from the whipping wind. The middle-aged woman named Bonni looked patient enough, but Colin was clearly a handful. His little face flushed with excitement Lisette didn't share, he clapped his hands at the thudding sound of hooves that made her turn back around in the saddle.

Her heart leapt to her throat to see Conall riding up to her, his gaze intense as he veered his spirited roan stallion around and reached out his hand to her.

"I want you with me, Lady Campbell. We'll go through the gates together."

Lisette blinked at him, not fully comprehending his intention until he leaned over and pulled her atop his horse, settling her between his thighs.

Her head spun from the abruptness of what he'd done and she must have gasped, but he only laughed with a deep, rich sound that thrilled her—she couldn't deny it! She loved the man with all her heart no matter the doubts and fears plaguing her.

His arms felt steely around her as he urged the stallion into a gallop that brought them back to the head of their entourage.

Her bottom wedged so tightly between his muscled thighs that she had no fear of falling, his warm breath fanning her cheek when he bent down his head to whisper in her ear.

"I can imagine what you've been thinking, wife, but *never* forget I love you. Only you and no other."

He pressed a fervent kiss to her burning face and then straightened and once again became the formidable warrior. His body grown tense as he guided his horse to just in front of the gates thrown open for them, his voice raised above the whistling wind.

"I claim this castle as my own at the behest of Robert, King of Scots!"

A great roar greeted his pronouncement from the warriors behind him and all those looking down from the fortress walls, men whooping and lifting high their weapons as Conall rode first through the gates.

Lisette's eyes widened not at a bailey ravaged by battle, but at the orderliness that greeted them.

The ground freshly swept and wooden barrels for fresh water lined up in neat rows alongside the walls. More warriors—at least forty, Lisette counted—assembled and awaiting them at attention with their plaid breacans fluttering in the wind, while those atop the walls scrambled down steep stone steps to join them. If she had been lacking in excitement before, now Lisette felt overwhelmed with exhilaration and pride as Conall acknowledged a russet-haired giant who had stepped forward, grinning.

"Finlay MacLachlan!"

"Aye, Conall, did you think Gabriel would send anyone other than one of his most trusted captains tae get this heap of stones ready for your arrival?"

Conall gave a laugh and clasped the Highlander's outstretched hand, the two men clearly friends, and then straightened to address everyone there.

"My thanks, kinsmen—MacLachlans and Campbells alike! We've food aplenty in the wagons tae prepare a fine feast. Let's gather tonight in the hall and enjoy a warming fire and supper together!"

His invitation was greeted with hearty shouts of approval while Finlay's gaze settled upon Lisette, his eyes crinkling at the corners as he smiled kindly at her.

"You've done well for yourself, Conall. Welcome, Lady Campbell. It seems tae be raining brides what with Gabriel and his Maggie, Cameron and Aislinn, and now another bonny lass tae grace us with her presence. We hope your wife is pleased with our efforts tae ensure her comfort. We usually wield swords, but we're handy as well with a broom and mop bucket, aye, men?"

A resounding "Aye!" went up that made Conall laugh again, his ease and good humor with them as their laird and commander making all those assembled laugh, too.

Yet the hilarity soon turned into an orderly hubbub when he urged his horse deeper into the bailey so the rest of his men and the wagons could enter the gates. At once everyone set to work unloading provisions and assisting the servants to disembark while others already a part of the household rushed from the keep to lend a hand.

Out of the corner of her eye, Lisette saw Father Philip dismount and say a word or two to the stoutest of the maidservants, who Aislinn had said wished to accompany them. A dark-haired woman with thick forearms and a sturdy build, she murmured something back to him and then they quickly parted and went their own ways.

The serving woman hastening toward the keep while the priest gave his horse over to a stable boy and then stood there awkwardly as if awaiting an invitation to enter himself.

"Aye, Father, go on with you!" Conall called out to him. "Find the chapel and see if it's tae your liking."

With a nod, the priest hurried after the serving woman, the two of them disappearing inside just as Conall brought his stallion right up to the entrance doors.

He still held Lisette so closely as if reluctant to release her, but then he dismounted and helped her down to stand in front of him.

"Welcome tae your new home, wife."

The husky emphasis on the last word made Lisette blush to her roots and he appeared about to kiss her. Yet an excited squeal made them both turn around to see Colin running up to Conall to grab him around the knees. The boy looked up...way up again at the father he already adored, and pointed with rounded eyes full of curiosity.

"What's on your head, Papa?"

Conall's laughter was deep and resonant as he pulled off the chain mail coif and bent down to show it to Colin. "Armor tae protect me in battle. Would you like tae hold it?"

Colin nodded, but he gasped when Conall gave him the coif, which was so heavy that the chain mail dropped with a chinking sound into the dirt. He glanced up at Conall again, looking doubtful this time.

"Did it make your head hurt?"

"No, but that's enough questions for now. Shall we go inside and look for your new bedchamber?"

Colin grabbed Lisette's hand with eagerness and then his father's hand, and they lifted him up over the pile of chain mail and swung him toward the doors opened wide.

The nursemaid not far behind, Colin's giggles ringing around them.

A family, Lisette found herself thinking with immense gratitude, though her earlier heartache wasn't yet forgotten.

Mayhap once she and Conall were finally alone, his kisses would help to erase that awful memory...

CHAPTER 18

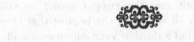

"By God, will we never be done with this accursed quest? Conall Campbell and his wife gone further north tae a heavily fortified castle by the sea?"

Isabeau held her tongue as Euan raged from the unexpected news they had just received from a MacDougall clansman, and paced like a caged beast upon the narrow deck. She had learned from their short marriage that it was better to stand back until the worst of his displeasure was past—or else she would bear the brunt of it.

She despised him so deeply for every slap, every pull of her hair, but mostly for the times he'd thrown her upon a bed and soothed his temper with his degrading possession of her that made her stomach roil at the thought.

The worst of it, though, was that there was no one to pity her.

Claudia, her mother, would have demanded the marriage annulled by the Church at the first letter from Isabeau describing her wretched existence as Lady MacCulloch. Yet there was no help from Normandy, her mother moldering in the Charpentier family graveyard.

God help her, Isabeau didn't want to even consider it, but Lisette would have pitied her—her sweet and kind half-sister who for all the misery she'd suffered at Isabeau's and her mother's hands, had rarely voiced a protest. Odd, how it had never occurred to her until now with Euan turning his blazing eyes upon her and his big hands clenched into fists.

"This wretched misadventure would never have happened if you hadna deceived me, wife! If you hadna schemed tae keep those jewels all tae yourself instead of sharing them with me, the *rightful* owner as your wedded laird. For all we know, the hem of that cloak has torn by now and a third of your inheritance spilled out into the hands of your bastard sister and that traitorous Highlander she married. Aye, mayhap a goodly portion gifted already tae Robert the Bruce tae support the murder of Scotsmen loyal tae England and the confiscation of their lands—och, Isabeau, I could kill you for your treachery and no one would fault me for it!"

He took a few menacing steps toward her while Isabeau backed away, her bottom coming up against the side of the ship.

There was nowhere to run unless she threw herself overboard, but she wouldn't give him the satisfaction. Instead she lifted her chin and faced him squarely, hoping that calm reason would quiet his rage.

"You've no need to fear that the hem has given way, husband, the garment triple stitched by one of the most skilled seamstresses to prevent such a mishap. There's little chance of the jewels being detected, either. Each one was wrapped in padding before being inserted into the hem—

and we'll regain the cloak soon enough if we sail at once to the north. You heard the man who brought us this news, *oui*? He said the journey is only a few hours overland and even swifter by sea."

Euan nodded though his face was still swarthy with fury, Isabeau taking heart that he seemed to be considering her words as she rushed on.

"You've two spies that managed to accompany them, both clever and resourceful enough to insert themselves into this new household and find a way to see the thing done. Yet here we still are with an hour at least until dusk. We've time enough to sail a good distance before dark and we'll have the light of the moon and even torches to guide us further—"

"Aye, beacons tae draw down upon us cold-blooded raiders that ply these waters—*woman, are you mad?*"

His incredulous bellow silencing her, Isabeau swallowed at the hard glitter in his eyes that truly frightened her...and heightened her deadly resolve to be rid of him as soon as she found the right moment. Taking a risky gamble, she lifted her chin higher and stared right back at him, defiant.

"Mayhap if such a ship comes upon us, you can make a bargain with them to help us in our quest. Half the jewels for safe passage to the castle and then southward to Dumfries, *non*, mayhap only a quarter or a third will be enough. You would know best how to haggle with such men if we encountered them...but there's always a chance that luck will remain with us, Euan, and we'll come and go with no one the wiser!"

He grunted as if still not convinced, but gestured for her to continue, Isabeau's mind working fast.

"No enemies have yet come upon us and the Mac-Dougalls will give you aid in whatever way you need, surely. They know this region where Lisette has gone. Bring some of those clansmen aboard to guide us to a secluded place where we can drop anchor—and then send them out to watch for when your spies leave the fortress. They'll make their move soon, they must! You see, husband? It's all not as impossible as it may seem—"

"You'd best pray it is so."

Isabeau felt a shiver at the ominous tone in Euan's voice, but he turned to confer with some of his men standing off to one side and didn't see her edging away to the other end of the ship.

For now, she wanted to stay as far away from him as possible, but she knew what would happen as soon as they set sail.

He would grab her arm and thrust her inside the tent, for he had already proclaimed a dozen times that the surging of the waves only heightened his pleasure. Mayhap this night would be different, though, with so much at stake and time slipping through their fingers.

Isabeau wasn't a woman for prayer, far from it. She nonetheless murmured a fervent entreaty that the young man posing as a priest as well as that stout maidservant would devise a way to procure the cloak and find a way out of the fortress before nightfall tomorrow.

She didn't care, either, if heaven or hell answered her.

Yet something told her as the MacDougall clansman who had brought them the wretched news came aboard along with two of his kinsmen—Euan shouting for the oars to be lowered—that it would probably be the latter.

"Does our new home please you, lass?"

Lisette bobbed her head, a shiver of anticipation coursing through her to hear Conall call her "lass" in his husky Scottish brogue.

They sat together on a bench in front of the immense hearth, most of the great hall cleared out but for servants carrying to the kitchen the last remnants of the evening meal...which had proved a boisterous occasion.

Somehow Finlay had discovered that the abundant provisions supplied by Cameron and Aislinn had been intended for a wedding feast, so the huge Highlander had seen to it that Lisette and Conall were so honored.

She could not believe that the cook and his helpers could have turned out so sumptuous a meal within a few hours' time, but they had done so with heaping platters of roasted venison and braised mutton on every table.

Savory side dishes of cooked vegetables and a thick barley stew flavored with leeks, garlic, and spices had been served alongside, as well as crusty loaves of bread, the fresh-baked aroma filling the air. Cups had been filled to the brim with ale or wine—Lisette wondering with a small hiccough if mayhap she had imbibed a bit too much—and the meal made complete with pear tart sweetened with honey and studded with dried cherries that Colin had especially enjoyed.

After eating so filling a supper, the sleepy little boy had been taken off to bed by his nursemaid, though it had been Conall who had filled his son's plate and given him the tiniest sip of ale, Colin smacking his lips and demanding more.

That had set the entire hall to laughing, and the merriment had continued for another hour or so with Finlay offering a congratulatory toast that other warriors soon followed with their own. Some flowery and some ribald, which had left Lisette blushing and Conall squeezing her hand and chuckling.

He clasped her hand now, absently playing with her fingers as they both stared into the fire. Another hiccough escaped from Lisette that made her gasp with chagrin.

"Too much wine, wife?" he teased her, while she could only nod truthfully, which made him give a low laugh though he seemed to grow serious of a sudden.

The next thing Lisette knew, he had gathered her into the crook of his arm to gaze down at her, his eyes darkened to the deepest blue in the firelight.

"I know you saw Lorna throw her arms around me and kiss me...but it was all her doing and not mine, wife. She wanted tae hurt you and stoke doubt in your heart, and I think mayhap she succeeded, aye?"

Again, Lisette could but nod for she wouldn't lie to him no matter that she could see a flicker of hurt in his gaze. She reached up to touch his face, feeling terrible about the fears that had plagued her during the journey, but it was done and she could not change it. All she could do was tell him how sorry she felt...so sorry.

"Forgive me, Conall, please—"

"Shh, love, *I* should be the one tae ask your forgiveness. I should have spoken tae you in the bailey and allayed your fears, but Cameron wanted us gone and on our way. I should have told you that Lorna will never see Colin again until he's grown into a man and can decide for himself if he wishes his mother in his life."

"Truly?"

"Aye, for you, Lisette, anything. I thought you would understand after how she treated you so unkindly that her display of affection was only a ruse tae distress you —and it worked, damn her. She's not the woman I knew years ago...though mayhap she is and I just didna see it then—och, men are a foolhardy lot and I'm one of them!"

Lisette blinked at Conall's exasperation with himself and then laughed, not out of humor but that he had just endeared himself to her so completely.

"Kiss me, husband...and help me to forget that it was Lorna's lips you last tasted—*oh!*"

Conall had crushed her against him in such a fierce hug that Lisette felt she couldn't breathe, but then he released her enough so she could look up at him.

His eyes staring into hers.

Her eyes staring into his.

Such emotion on his face that she felt her heartbeat race even as he lowered his head to kiss her for the longest moment...the most wondrous moment, until she was sighing against his mouth, her hands cradling his face.

A face roughened with stubble that nonetheless thrilled her at the wanton thought of his cheek brushing against her breasts while he savored first one hardened nipple and then the other—

"I think it's well past time we retire tae our bed-chamber, aye, lass?"

Lass! She could hear him call her that a hundred times, a thousand times with a husky burr that sounded more a sweet endearment, Lisette nodding her head.

Her face flushed. Her hands trembling as he rose and lifted her up easily beside him, and then picked up the cloak draped over the bench to wrap it around her shoulders.

His arm winding around her waist to guide her from the great hall cast in a flickering glow from torches set high upon the stone pillars soaring to the ceiling.

Yet if that sight seemed enchanting, Conall pausing to kiss her a half dozen times before they stepped outside into the cool air, the sky filled with twinkling stars was truly a wonder to behold.

The great hall hadn't been constructed as part of the keep, but a separate building that Lisette was grateful for so they would have more time to enjoy the night.

"Are you warm enough?" Conall murmured against her hair, stopping to draw her in front of him and embrace her as he kissed her forehead, her temple, and the warmth of her cheek. "You must be, Lisette, I can feel you blushing."

She *was* blushing, so enthralled by his kisses, the stirring sound of his voice, and the strength of his arms around her that she couldn't speak for the emotion swelling within her heart.

The glittering stars across the vast expanse of sky,

the distant sound of waves crashing, the cool night breeze lifting her hair, the woodsy masculine scent of Conall as he held her close, his eyes appearing black in the glow of torches sputtering around the bailey...all of it she would remember as long as she lived.

Her heart racing and with all the love she possessed, she stood slightly on tiptoes and pressed her mouth to his lips, whispering against them, "*Je t'aime,* Conall...*aujourd'hui, demain, et pour toujours.*"

He kissed her back, though she sensed confusion in him that made him lift his head to look at her as if he hadn't understood what she said. He was so handsome, so dear...and she laughed softly, her cheeks firing anew.

"I love you, Conall...today, tomorrow, and for always."

His breath seemed to catch as if he couldn't believe what she had just said, his expression boyish in its wonder.

"I heard you say some of those words last night...but I thought I'd dreamed it. Say them again, Lisette—"

"*Je t'aime,*" she broke in softly, reaching up again to caress his face. "I love you."

"*Je...t'aime...*" he repeated slowly as if accustoming himself to the cadence of her language, his tender smile making her heart feel full to breaking. "I love you..."

Conall looked so vulnerable at that moment, so unlike the hardened warrior of only hours ago that Lisette swore to herself she would never again doubt him.

She would never again allow fear to darken their life together. She felt so ashamed still, but as if sensing her thoughts, he swept her up into his arms and whirled with her in the middle of the bailey until her head spun.

He threw back his head and whooped, and she did, too, some of the guards on duty rushing forward to see if anything was amiss—only for Conall to stop and smile broadly at them.

"My wife loves me!"

"Laird?" queried one man, casting a look at the guard beside him, and then he smiled, too, chuckling. "Aye, a bountiful marriage tae you both and bairns aplenty!"

"Bairns aplenty..." Conall echoed, hugging Lisette closer as he strode with her toward the keep. "Bairns aplenty, wife, did you hear the man? I'd say we've been wasting time gazing at the stars, aye?"

"Aye, husband, aye," she murmured, burying her burning face into his neck as her heartbeat quickened at what lay ahead.

Conall had begun to laugh and she giggled with him, too, the keep ringing with their joy as he raced up the steps, two at a time.

CHAPTER 19

"**D**o you see a flag, man?"

"No, Laird, the torchlight aboard their ship is too dim. They're under full sail, though, and flying upon the waves—"

"*Lunacy*! If the shallow depth doesna destroy their hull, then the rocks ahead will—by God, look! Whoever has their hands upon the helm must know these waters well tae change their course so abruptly. Keep us well within sight of their ship, but not so close that they'll see us. The night is dark enough no matter the quarter moon, so we should be able tae shadow them, aye?"

"Aye, like a wraith out of the mouth of hell. They dinna call you the devil of the seas for no good reason!"

Gavin MacLachlan scowled at his helmsman's cackling, but the unknown ship was too far away for the sound to carry above the whistling wind filling their own sail.

The thick cloth dyed a red ochre that wasn't as easy to spot as the white sail on the other vessel, especially at night. The deck and mast and stowed oars were stained black, and the hull blackened with tar, which added to their cover. Their tunics and breacans were black, too, so they did look a demon ship straight out of

Hades when coming upon unsuspecting vessels ripe for plunder.

With the sail billowing and salt spray stinging his face, Gavin felt that same familiar thrill of exhilaration whenever he and his men were on the hunt.

An exhilaration fueled by fierce emotion—fury and a burning lust for retribution—that wracked him as well and made his hands clench tightly into fists.

He towered over the wiry helmsman, Gavin's feet spread wide for balance and the wind whipping at his shoulder-length hair. A dark red that had been likened to the color of blood melded with fire as captive sailors had vomited in fear before they were thrown overboard to swim for their lives to shore.

He had never wantonly killed anyone if unarmed, but in battle upon the sea with swords flashing, aye, plenty had felt the deadly swipe of his blade.

He was a raider with any ship fair game for plundering if he judged he could take it, and some he allowed to continue empty of goods to a home port. Yet if the vessel they shadowed proved English, Gavin would burn it to ashes upon the waves.

He hated England for the oppression and brutality of its late king, Edward, his weakling son now upon the throne. That wretched oppression had divided Scotland, many loyal to England for the royal favor bestowed upon them while others sought clan alliances to enrich their power, which had been at the heart of Gavin losing the woman he loved.

Cora.

Gavin swore under his breath. She was never far from his mind, but he forced himself to focus upon their quarry. Was the ship coursing ahead of them part of some planned invasion? If so, then where was the rest of the fleet? Again Gavin scanned the dark sea, but there was no sign of other sails as far as he could peer into the distance.

He usually sailed the waters closer to England, where the pickings were more numerous and richer, and even as far south as the coast of Normandy, where he had spent the last few months. Aye, he despised the French, too, with their duplicitous lust for alliances with England, their long-hated enemy.

A seething web of pacts and agreements that had stomped the hearts and hopes of countless victims into dust and despair and heartache—like what had happened to him and the woman he had wanted to marry, *Cora*!

The only reason Gavin had ventured this close to Argyll, a place he had sworn never to return to again, was because he'd heard startling news that had spurred him northward.

He had been long at sea until a week past, having returned from France, and had docked his loaded ship near Dumfries where he had traded plunder for gold coin—the ruthless men he dealt with asking no questions.

Most of the talk in the seedy inn had been of King Edward's death and his son's fondness for male lovers, and whether this younger Edward would have courage enough to carry on his father's quest to subdue Scotland. The discourse had then turned to foul curses against the false king, Robert the Bruce, and how he had narrowly escaped death at the hands of Seoras Mac-Dougall when one of the earl's own men had risen up against him and lopped off his head.

Gabriel MacLachlan, Gavin's own cousin! He had scarcely heard anything else for his heartbeat roaring in his ears.

Cora...a widow. Even now he found it hard to believe as his helmsman pointed into the darkness, their quarry steering closer to the shore.

"Mayhap they're planning tae anchor for the rest of

the night, Laird. Shall I draw closer and we prepare for battle?"

"No, we'll wait until daybreak and see if they're staying or bound elsewhere. Steer us tae shore as well, but with a good distance between us so they dinna suspect we're near."

"Aye, Laird!"

Gavin left the helmsman's side and went to the railing to peer into the distance at the ship's sputtering torches that one by one, were being extinguished. Further away and rising above a promontory was a walled fortress where lights shone, though he didn't know what laird resided there. The last he knew, it had been a Mac-Dougall, but if Seoras had been overthrown and slain, then mayhap others in that clan had met the same fate.

Gavin's men called him laird as well, but he owned no castle or land—only the ship surging beneath his feet. He had stolen an eight-oar fishing boat to sail away from Argyll, his first plunder as a raider, and within a few weeks had traded for another vessel, and then another until he'd gained this thirty-two oared birlinn that glided like a sleek serpent through the waves.

His hatred growing all the while for those responsible for tearing Cora away from him...Earl Seoras and her clan, the Campbells.

Where had she gone after her husband had been killed? Back to her family's home? He would not rest until he found her...God help him that she wasn't already wed again.

If their quarry proved to be English, he would destroy them and resume his journey to the furthest reaches of Argyll where he had first set eyes upon Cora.

If a Scots ship, mayhap he would let them go, but his gut instincts told him some treachery must be afoot for a ship to travel at night with torches lighting their way...risking raiders such as himself to come upon them.

Fools! Soon he would know...

~

"Will you wake and see me off, lass?" Conall's whisper did no more than make Lisette's eyelids flutter. She snuggled in her sleep even closer to him, her warm nakedness making him groan.

He would never quench his desire for her—*never*! Their lovemaking had carried them deep into the night, so it was no wonder that he could not rouse her, but there were other ways to coax her from her slumber.

She smiled and even laughed softly as if delighted by a dream, which made Conall hesitate now to wake her though he knew he had only moments more to linger.

Her tousled head against his shoulder and her curled hand beneath her chin, her breath like a sweet whisper across his chest, which made him groan again.

His wife. His forever love.

Yet what was the most wondrous revelation of all— she loved him, too. She had told him last night after she'd collapsed satiated against him, her silken thighs straddling his hips and his hands still clutching her perfectly rounded bottom...that she had known she loved him from the moment they had consummated their marriage.

She had stared down at him with such emotion in her eyes, tears glimmering in her lashes that had dropped like warm raindrops upon his face...the taste of salt upon his lips when she had bent her head to kiss him.

Och, how was he to leave her now with such stirring thoughts making him want desperately to stay? Yet Gabriel had ordered him and Cameron to make a display of might to all residing upon their lands—clansmen loyal to King Robert as well as the MacDougalls no doubt plotting to do harm if presented with a chance.

That stark reality alone was enough to make Conall rouse Lisette with a gentle shake.

He wanted to look into her eyes before he rose from their bed to dress and then meet his men in the bailey —half of them to remain behind to guard the castle while the rest would ride out with him across the countryside.

Their first stop would be the village they had passed a quarter league away, the windows shuttered and doors closed though Conall knew the residents were hiding inside. He didn't blame them given his show of force yesterday, but he wanted everyone to understand that he wished to live peaceably with them so they all could prosper.

The weather had turned cooler already as the summer was fading and harvest time coming, and Conall had seen that the golden fields were heavy with oats and barley that would tide them all through the winter.

As baron, he would share the bounty with his tenants gladly, but he demanded loyalty from each and every one of them—all this they would soon know. Yet it wouldn't happen with him whiling away the morning with Lisette, no matter how much he wished to remain by her side.

"Wake, wife...you must wake."

This time she seemed to hear his voice and stretched languorously against him, which made Conall wish again that he could remain abed as she opened her eyes to gaze upon him.

Her rosy lips curving into a gentle smile that filled his heart with such love for this woman that his breath caught at the wonder of it. Lisette reached out to trace a finger along his stubbly cheek and then she cradled his face and drew him down to kiss her.

A long, languid kiss that made his lower body grow hard and a chuckle escape him that she could rouse him so easily—by God, if he didn't jump out of bed now, he would never leave her!

He did, too, Lisette gasping as he threw aside the covers and swung his legs over the side of the bed to rise and pad on bare feet away from her...though everything in him wanted to rush back and kiss her again.

"Must you leave me, husband?"

Her soft query an agony to him, Conall nodded and thrust his arms through his tunic and then drew it over his head.

"You know I canna stay...but my men and I will return by dusk. Will you look in upon Colin? Mayhap we'll need two nursemaids tae keep up with him, aye?"

His query drew a laugh from her as she rose naked from the bed.

He stopped pulling on a boot and stared at her loveliness. The creamy perfection of her breasts and the tempting curve of her hips made his loins tighten again, Conall wanting nothing more than to cast off his clothes and toss her back onto the rumpled sheets.

Somehow he forced himself to focus upon his other boot and then his sword belt, followed by a quick tunneling of his fingers through his own tousled hair and he was done.

Lisette had hastily dressed, too, in a lavender gown and with her cloak wrapped around her, for it was clear she intended to accompany him down into the bailey to see him off.

"So you did hear me the first time," he said as she ran an intricately carved comb, which Aislinn must have given her, through her long dark tresses.

Lisette's soft giggle in response told him that it had been her purpose to ignore him so they might have a few more moments in bed together, which made him draw close to pull her into his arms.

The wooden comb dropping to the floor with a clatter.

Lisette sighing when he kissed her, gently at first but then so passionately that he seemed to surprise her.

He knew from many battles that life was precious and could be lost in an instant, though he held no fear of not returning to her. Yet mayhap he wanted to reassure her, Lisette's arms flying around him to hug him as tightly.

"You and Colin will be safe here," he said against her lips, and then he lifted his head to look down at her. "I'm leaving Finlay in command of the fortress while I'm gone. You can trust him as I trust him. Now we must go."

As he released Lisette to clasp her hand and draw her along with him to the door, Conall could hear through the closed shutters the commotion outside of whinnying horses and riders assembling.

The square keep had no glass windows like Cameron's fortress and no towers either, both of which Conall intended to remedy to make this castle as comfortable as he could for Lisette and Colin.

He wanted her to be able to stand in their bedchamber and look out over the sea without rain or wind to deter her. For the children they would have together, the added room a tower or two would afford them was a necessity, to his mind.

He had so many ambitious plans springing up inside him for the present, the future...for their life together within these walls and for the lands he had been granted. He would never have imagined such responsibility for himself only a few months ago, but he would no more fail his new family than King Robert.

As if sensing his thoughts, Lisette's cheeks were flushed pink and her eyes danced with excitement as she squeezed his hand and flew down the steps with him—but she sobered as soon as they stepped outside into the chilly morning air.

The cloudless sky was only now lightening with

streaks of pink and orange, casting her in an ethereal glow that took his breath away.

He wanted to tell her that he loved her and that she was beautiful...his life blessed beyond measure to have her as his wedded wife, but Finlay striding up to them broke the spell with his great booming voice.

"All is in readiness, Conall!"

"I hear you, man," he replied with a wry smile, letting go of Lisette's hand. He strode away from her without a backward glance; otherwise, he doubted he would find the will to leave her.

Only when he had mounted his roan stallion and veered the animal around to face the keep did Conall see that Lisette had retreated inside as if she, too, couldn't bear to be parted from him.

No fond words.

No last kiss—och, it was better this way, he told himself, waving his arm for his men to follow him as he rode through the gates flung wide.

As he had told her, he would return by dusk, Conall already counting the minutes until he once again held her in his arms.

CHAPTER 20

"Was it wise to send them out last night to find horses? It could raise an alarm—"

"They're MacDougalls!" Euan snapped at Isabeau as the three men waded out of the shallow water toward the horses they'd left tethered in the trees along the shoreline. "That village must be filled with their kinsmen, so no one would dare utter a word. Be glad they know this region, just as you said. Soon they'll be hiding outside the castle and awaiting our spies tae make their move—aye, mayhap this morning, I can sense it."

Did her husband sense, too, how much she hated him? Clenching her teeth, Isabeau turned away with the thought of taking refuge in their tent for now they faced more waiting—*mon Dieu*! If there wasn't such a fortune of jewels sewn into that cloak, she would have demanded already for them to steer the ship homeward—

"Laird MacCulloch, there's a vessel coming upon us! Aye, a raider for certain with that blood red sail!"

The helmsman's terrified cry making the hair prickle at the back of her neck, Isabeau spun around to see that Euan's face had blanched white. He nonetheless waved onward the three clansmen who had stopped in their tracks upon the shore, and they quickly mounted the horses and disappeared into the trees as if they had never been there.

"Take up your weapons—but do nothing unless I command you!" he shouted to the sailors who scrambled to obey him, while Isabeau hastened to his side—not feeling terrified at all, but strangely exhilarated.

"Don't forget my suggestion to you, husband—we can bargain with them! With such riches soon to be ours, they would be fools to harm us."

Somehow Isabeau's words rang hollow to her at closer sight of the vessel, every inch stained black but for the ominous sail billowing in the wind.

In truth, there was nowhere they could escape to and it was too late to draw up the anchor and push away from shore with the oars.

The ship had come out of nowhere as if a phantom, yet mayhap they had simply been waiting nearby for dawn to break before attacking. Those accursed torches! Wishing now that she had never suggested their use, Isabeau lifted her chin as the ship drew closer...closer...her heart near to pounding from her breast.

It wasn't as much out of fear...but that the most magnificent man she had ever seen stood at the prow with his dark red hair flying behind him.

Tall, strapping, and built as strongly as the Vikings of yore that had conquered Normandy centuries before...*oui*, she was even descended from them!

A fearsome sword in his right hand glinting in the first bright rays of sunlight.

His men were fully armed, too, from what Isabeau could see with the ship aimed straight at them as if the raider intended to ram their vessel into splinters. Only within the last moments was the sail expertly furled while others took to the oars to bring the ship in closer to them, Euan shouting for her to hide herself in the tent.

She ignored him...nothing on earth to tear her away from whatever was to come. She stared open-mouthed as the man appeared even more breathtakingly handsome now that he stood only fifteen feet away aboard his ship.

She had never fancied red hair on a man, but this fearsome raider deserved an exception for truly, he was beautiful.

"Scots or English?" he bellowed with a deep, menacing voice that gave Isabeau shivers.

"*Scots!*" she cried out at the same time as Euan, who threw her a black look as if expecting her to hold her tongue.

Yet how could she with so formidable a man appraising her from head to toe? Glad that she had dressed that morning in a sapphire blue gown that complemented her dark hair and eyes, Isabeau blushed deeply—*her, blushing!*—as visions of him taking her in his muscled arms to ravage her flew through her mind.

The next thing she knew, the raider's men had pulled in their oars and stowed them beneath the oar holes so the ship now flanked their vessel. With one lunge, he jumped from his deck onto their deck with his sword brandished and a dozen of his men swarming behind to join him.

"Drop your weapons if you wish tae live!"

Thuds all around greeted the raider's command, Isabeau realizing then from his thick brogue that he was a Scotsman, too. God help her, she couldn't wait to be free of Euan, the lust she felt for this man overwhelming her.

If all went as she hoped and he agreed to their bargain, she would find him again one day, she swore it! What a glorious time they would share as lovers with a wealth in precious jewels between them...

"Name your purpose for anchoring here!" demanded the raider. "Are you staying or moving onward?"

She almost answered again for Euan, but he waved her angrily to silence.

"We're on a mission and soon tae be on our way," her husband sought to explain, gesturing to the castle atop the promontory no more than a quarter league away. "We've no quarrel with you and ask that you leave us in peace—"

"You *ask*?" scoffed the raider, his men fanning out to every corner of the ship and guffawing with laughter. "You're in no position tae ask me anything, Laird...?"

"MacCulloch...from Dumfries."

"Och, then, an enemy of King Robert, if you hail from that town. What could be so crucial tae make you sail at night with torches lighting your way? Didna you think that raiders such as myself would spy you?"

"*Oui, monsieur*, but it was worth it to us—and mayhap worth much to you as well if you'll only hear us!" Isabeau interjected, Euan glowering at her now with his fists clenched. "We seek something stolen from me and we'll gladly share it with you if you agree to accompany us safely home. I'm sure my husband will offer you an added reward once we reach Dumfries, won't you, Euan?"

If a look could strike one dead, Isabeau would have taken her last breath at that moment, though her husband nodded slowly and turned back to the raider.

"Do you have a name? It would help tae know it as we make our bargain..."

The man's sardonic laughter silenced Euan, who had blanched again though Isabeau found herself enjoying every moment just to see his discomfort.

"Aye, I have a name. Helmsman! What do they call me?"

The wiry fellow that skittered to the side of the raider's ship laughed, too, a high-pitched cackle bordering on madness that unnerved Isabeau—and only then did she feel a niggling of raw fear.

"Devil of the seas, Laird! *Devil of the seas*!"

~

Lisette hurried up the steps of the keep with a tray she had prepared for Colin's breakfast, his room down the hall from the one she shared with Conall.

Their bedchambers situated on the second story of the massive structure, with two more floors above them and an attic, she had been told by the servants already hard at work in the kitchen. She still knew so little of the household, but she was grateful for the task ahead of her. Anything to keep her busy whenever Conall was away, her heart aching that he had left her so soon.

She knew the duties of a baron were many and he was bound by honor to attend to King Robert's wishes —but why couldn't they have lingered together in bed for just a little while longer this morning?

Their first morning in their new home—ah, God, but she was a warrior's wife and must become accustomed to these separations. Some only for a day, as Conall had said he would return by dusk, and some that would stretch out for weeks and months if he was ever called upon by the king to leave Argyll to join him in battle.

It could happen—and most likely *would* happen— but for now Lisette took comfort in that she only had mere hours to fill before they were together again.

The servants stoking the ovens and preparing the morning meal for those warriors who had remained behind and everyone else in the household had been startled, indeed, to see her enter their domain. All she had wanted was a steaming bowl of porridge for Colin and a cup of goat's milk, which would be enough to nourish the boy until midday.

She had considered a round of things for them to do together, but mayhap he simply wanted to play in his room with the wooden toys Aislinn and Sorcha had given him to add to the few that Lorna had brought with them from Perthshire.

Even now, it pained her to think of the woman and how she had so cruelly chosen to torment her—but that was in the past, another reason for her to feel comforted.

Her beloved husband had seen to it that Lorna would not trouble her again, which made Lisette's heart lighter as she reached the second story and hurried past her bedchamber.

Already maidservants had entered the room to tidy it and fix the bed, making her blush at what they must think to have found it in so disheveled a condition. She heard feminine voices and giggles, which answered her question, Lisette rushing past the door with the cloak swirling around her feet.

The air felt as chilled as Cameron and Aislinn's keep, which made her grateful again for the garment's warmth. She hastened toward Colin's room, but was surprised to see the door was yawning open.

Strange, considering he should still be sleeping, Lisette looking forward to waking him and seeing those big blue eyes and his happy smile. She imagined the nursemaid who slept on a cot in the same bedchamber must have stepped out for a moment, an eerie silence greeting Lisette when she walked in with the tray.

Colin's bed was empty, the covers thrown back, but it was the feet sticking out from the opposite side on the floor that made Lisette's heart lurch into her throat.

One shoe on and the other bare...

"Bonni?" she whispered, wondering if the kindly and ever patient nursemaid was playing an early morning game with Colin. Hide-and-seek, surely, but why then did the woman's legs looked sprawled out as if she had fallen? Lisette ventured closer and peeked around the side of the bed...horror filling her at the sight of the unconscious woman with an ugly purple bump on her forehead.

"Oh, no...oh, no," she murmured, her hands shaking as she set the tray upon the mattress, but it was the soft intake of breath behind her that made Lisette whirl around.

Her knees nearly giving way at the sight of Colin held tightly behind the door by the stout serving maid Lisette had seen speaking to the priest yesterday in the bailey, the woman's large hand covering the boy's mouth.

"Dinna scream, Lady Campbell, or the child dies. I could take your cloak now but they'll not open the gates for me or Father Philip. There's only way one for us tae leave the fortress and that's together."

"Cloak?" Lisette echoed, glancing down in confusion at the garment made especially for Isabeau and then back to the serving maid. "I-I don't understand—"

"No questions, it will all be made plain tae you as soon as we're out of this place. Now you'll walk with me quickly tae the bailey where Father Philip awaits us with a wagon. *Go!*"

The woman hadn't shouted, but the vehemence in that last word spurred Lisette into motion as Colin began to wriggle in the serving maid's arms.

What could she say to soothe him? She didn't know what was happening any more than the child, whose eyes filled with frightened tears. If he began to wail in spite of the hand pressed over his mouth, would the woman break his neck as easily as a twig with those thick forearms?

Seeing only malevolent determination in the serving maid's dark eyes, Lisette guessed that was exactly what would happen if Colin burst into loud sobs.

Pausing just outside the door and trembling from head to toe, she took a deep breath and turned around with her arms outstretched.

"Let me take him. I'll make it into a game...please."

The woman said nothing, but Lisette could see her mind working as if weighing the offer, and then abruptly shoved Colin toward her.

At once Lisette scooped him up, Colin throwing his arms around her neck and burying his face into her shoulder, but she forced a light laugh to try and calm him.

"We're going for a ride, Colin...would you like that?"

He nodded weakly, and lifted his head to look at her with his blue eyes brimming. "A-a ride?"

"*Oui*, in a wagon. You liked the wagon yesterday and the horses. We'll have fun, you'll see!"

Lisette felt swamping relief as Colin's clouded expression turned into a smile. Behind her, as they stepped into the hall, the serving woman stuck the point of something sharp against her back.

"Move!"

She did, Colin pretending to gallop in her arms that almost made her drop him, his giggles ringing around them at the high expectation of his wagon ride. Somehow Lisette made it past her own room where the maidservants glanced up from their work, shrugged, and then went back to fixing the bed—and finally to the steps where she almost faltered.

Again she felt the poke of what she guessed was a knife, which spurred her downward with the serving woman feigning laughter—a cruel sound that reminded Lisette of Lorna.

What could she do in the bailey? Shout for help? Scream out for Finlay? Yet she knew that she would do none of those things if it meant risking Colin's life.

It seemed another moment and the brisk morning air hit her face again when they stepped outside, but this time Lisette wasn't there to bid goodbye to Conall.

Just as the serving maid had said, Father Philip

awaited them with a wagon, his pale blue eyes narrowed in a visible threat.

"Climb in, we must go!"

He held out his arms for Colin and she could do nothing but lift the boy up to him, while the serving woman encircled Lisette's waist with her big hands and hoisted her bodily into the back of the wagon. Then she climbed in beside her while the priest, holding Colin fast upon his lap, flicked the reins at the same horse he had ridden yesterday, the wagon jerking into motion.

Lisette saw Conall's warriors who stood guard around the bailey turn startled faces toward them, while others on the battlements peered down to see the wagon heading straight for the gates.

Massive gates that were closed—while Finlay's raised voice carried to them from somewhere nearby.

"Lady Campbell? Conall said nothing tae me of your leaving the fortress. Is aught amiss?"

"Tell him tae let us out, or you'll both die!" shouted Father Philip, neither he nor the woman appearing to care now that Colin began to sob as if sensing the horror gripping Lisette.

She opened her mouth to speak, but already Finlay had lunged for the gates and was ordering them open, clearly having heard the priest.

All she could do was stare wide-eyed as they careened past him and a cluster of warriors with their hands upon the hilts of their swords, but what could they do?

The serving maid flashed her knife at them and then pressed it to Lisette's throat, the priest holding Colin so tightly that he wailed now in earnest.

A few blurred moments, Lisette's mind spinning, and they were well away from the castle walls as three riders burst out of the trees.

Their faces set grimly as the wagon jolted to a halt.

Lisette told herself that she should scream, or struggle, or do something as one of the men grabbed her and set her down hard in front of him while another seized Colin, the boy crying out in terror.

Yet the priest had no sooner jumped on behind the man holding Colin, the serving maid reaching out to the third rider who drew his snorting mount alongside her—when a whizzing sound came from the castle. The woman fell dead to the ground with an arrow sticking out of her back.

"*Ride!*" shouted the priest, but he was struck through the neck in a spray of blood by another arrow. Lisette watched in horror as he pitched sideways from the horse, nearly pulling Colin and the second man with him.

The boy's anguished cries ringing around them, the rider who had grabbed Lisette plunged his mount into the woods with Colin's captor right behind them— while a high-pitched scream told her that the man at the rear had been struck by an arrow, too.

She could only close her eyes as they careened through the trees at a breakneck pace...while a great roar went up from the direction of the castle, followed by the thundering of horses.

Finlay and some of Conall's men must be coming after them—please God, may it be so!

Yet the distance was already wide between them, Lisette having no idea where she and Colin were being taken.

Still their captors drove their horses with a relentless purpose, and she no longer knew how long they had been riding for the fear paralyzing her.

The cloak, the cloak! Why would the serving maid have mentioned taking it as if that was what they most wanted—and not her and Colin?

A terrible intuition began to grow inside her, but she had no more time to think when they burst out of the trees and onto a pebbly beach where two ships were anchored thirty feet from shore.

One an ominous black but for its red furled sail... while the other bore a dark-haired woman who rushed to the railing, a smug smile lighting her face.

Ah, God, no... *Isabeau*.

CHAPTER 21

"God help us, *Conall*!"

Finlay's outcry carrying to him over the distance still separating them, Conall didn't slow the hard pace of his mount until he was almost upon the Highlander and several other riders—all of their faces flushed with alarm.

He already knew something ominous was afoot from the tumult emanating from the castle that he'd heard all the way to the village, borne by the wind—but *what*?

Finlay wouldn't have ridden out from the fortress if they were under attack, which left Conall pulling up so hard on the reins that his stallion reared on its hind legs, squealing. Finlay didn't even blink but skirted the startled animal and veered his own mount around so he was alongside Conall.

"It's Lady Campbell and your son—they've been taken! Three of the bastards were slain outside the fortress and I sent men after the riders that disappeared into the woods skirting the sea. One with your wife and the other with Colin. They must have come by ship—"

"Ride, man, we must ride!" His gut twisting, his own face flushed hot with fury, Conall urged his stallion into a wild gallop that left the others thundering after him.

The warriors that had left the castle with him only a short while ago.

Finlay and his men.

A vengeful roar breaking from sixty throats.

From Conall's throat, too, the wind whistling in his ears and his heart pounding.

An overwhelming thought torturing him that he hadn't taken a moment to kiss Lisette before he had left the bailey.

One moment!

He hated himself then almost as much as whoever had taken them—*God protect his wife and child, please let him not be too late!*

~

Lisette stood shivering against the railing, Isabeau wrenching the sodden cloak from her shoulders as soon as her feet touched the deck.

Colin hugged her knees and wept inconsolably, the poor child soaked and shivering, too.

Their captors had driven their wheezing horses straight into the waves and ridden out to the ships, Lisette and Colin hauled aboard by black-clad men that appeared more brigands than sailors—and within another moment, she knew why.

A fearsome-looking man who stood taller than anyone else appeared to be in command. His feet spread wide and his hand clenching a sword as he roared out orders to what must be his own men and Euan MacCulloch's as well.

Lisette had never seen a raider before, but she had heard anxious talk of them on the voyage with Isabeau from Normandy to Dumfries—and she believed she was looking at one now.

His dark red hair blowing wild in the wind, his eyes an intense brown instead of the blue or green that she'd seen before with such coloring. His voice as harsh as his expression that made Lisette shiver even more violently.

"Lash the ships together!"

Men scrambled to obey him using thick ropes while Euan and Isabeau watched silently, the dripping burgundy cloak clutched by both of them. Lisette had never known her half-sister to look fearful, but if she'd been smiling moments before as if with triumph, now Isabeau glanced with uncertainty from the red-haired giant back to her husband's ashen face.

"Raise the anchors! Man the oars! My men tae starboard and MacCulloch's tae port—aye, and put your backs into it! *Row!*"

Again the men nearly fell over themselves to oblige him without question. The two ships moving together as one vessel away from shore and into deep water where no riders could hope to reach them without risk of drowning.

Helpless tears filled Lisette's eyes as behind them, the pounding of hooves grew louder until a host of men burst from the trees and onto the beach where they reined in their snorting mounts.

Roars of frustration laced with curses carried to them and made the raider smile grimly at the success of his strategy, but it faded when he turned his hard gaze upon Isabeau.

"You said you sought a cloak, Lady MacCulloch... not a woman and child."

Isabeau's nonchalant shrug only made his face grow ruddy with anger, Lisette standing closest to him and seeing a tic working along his clenched jaw.

"She's nothing...only my bastard half-sister. She stole the cloak from me—"

"I did not steal it!" Lisette hugged Colin more tightly, his sobs muffled as he had buried his face in her skirt. More thundering hooves could be heard and she glanced at the shoreline, but she didn't see Conall—ah, God, did he even know what had happened to her?

She was so focused upon scanning the men who sat infuriated atop their wheeling horses that she didn't realize the raider had approached her until she felt Colin flinch.

The man had cupped the boy's shoulder with a massive hand and turned him around as if to see him better, his own curse rending the air.

"Raven-black hair and blue eyes...a Campbell if ever I've seen one."

Lisette knew true fear then at the bitterness in his voice, but she threw her arm protectively around Colin to draw him back against her legs.

"*Oui*, he's Conall Campbell's son! King Robert awarded him that castle you see and made him a baron! He'll be here soon and he'll fight you—"

"*Fight me?* Does he walk on water? I knew Conall when we were boys. He was foolhardy then and from the sound of it, he hasna changed."

Stunned, Lisette could only stare at him while Isabeau rushed up between them, brandishing the soaking wet cloak that she had wrested away from her husband.

Euan stormed after her, but he stopped dead when the raider cast him a forbidding look that made his face turn pale.

"Stay where you are, MacCulloch, while I see this treasure that you wish tae share with me." The raider grabbed the cloak from Isabeau, who seemed ready to protest until he scowled at her so fiercely that she snapped her mouth shut.

A knife pulled from his belt flashed in the sunlight and then he ripped into the hem of the garment.

The rending sound followed by a dull pelting upon the deck, Lisette's eyes widening at the glittering stones lying there while Isabeau gave a triumphant laugh.

"My jewels at last! My mother told me they belonged to a sultan in the Holy Land—rubies, emeralds, and sapphires! Spoils of war from the Crusades—"

"Now *mine*, Lady MacCulloch. Did you truly think that bargaining with a man called the devil of the seas would bring you the outcome you desired?"

Isabeau's mouth had dropped open and she sputtered to find words while Euan gaped at him, his face flushing with fury.

*Devil of the sea*s.

Lisette gaped, too, astonished that the jewels had been sewn into the cloak that she'd worn all along without knowing.

What was to become of her and Colin with so ruthless a man holding their lives in his hands? The boy's sobs had quieted to a soft hiccoughing, but he shivered still and his lips were bluish—God help them!

She glanced again toward the shore, her heart sinking when she didn't see Conall among the warriors crowding the beach.

Their horses whinnied shrilly as some of the men urged them into the crashing waves—only to turn back when the skittish animals bucked and reared.

"Fools!" grated the raider. "If they have no ship, then there will be no fight."

"I will fight you!" Euan rushed at the man as if by sheer force he could knock him down, but the raider sidestepped him and Euan went crashing onto the deck. Yet instead of trying to get up, he scrambled on hands and knees to gather as many of the jewels as he could while Isabeau shrieked and fell to her knees beside him.

"No! They're mine! Give them to me—*give them to me!*"

Everything happened so fast, Isabeau reaching up to knock the knife from the raider's hand and grab the weapon to plunge it into Euan's neck—her husband collapsing onto the deck.

His arms and legs twitching convulsively as blood streamed from the wound and pooled beneath him.

A terrible rasping noise breaking from his throat as Euan gave one last shudder and then lay still, dead.

Staring in horror, Lisette scooped up Colin as Isabeau lunged to her feet, her dark eyes narrowed.

"You're the one to blame for this misery—I hate you! *Hate you!*"

The raider reached out to catch her arm, but he was too late, Isabeau crashing into Lisette and trying to push her overboard.

Colin wailing in terror. Lisette twisting to one side and holding desperately onto the railing as another shrill shriek rent the air.

Isabeau hoisted up bodily by the raider and pitched into the sea.

Lisette felt herself pulled safely away from the railing even as her half-sister flailed her arms and screamed for help.

Screamed that she couldn't swim.

Screamed in vain as the raider brandished his sword as if daring anyone to make a move.

Isabeau choking and sputtering and sinking beneath the waves until only her clawlike hands could be seen... and then they, too, disappeared.

With a vehement curse, the raider swept up the cloak and threw it into the sea where Isabeau had been only a moment before. Then he drew Lisette, weeping from the horror of it all, further away from the railing.

"Your tears are wasted on such a one."

She hiccoughed, trying to stop but unable to as Colin sobbed, too, his wet face buried against her neck. She had held him there so he wouldn't see what she'd seen, but he had heard it—ah, God, such a terrible day for one so young.

"K-King Robert sent Conall to abduct her on the eve of her m-marriage as revenge against Euan for executing his brothers," she babbled to the raider, not sure if he listened or not as he gestured for some of his men to pick up Euan's body. "C-Conall was to marry her, too, but he mistakenly took me instead. We wed the next day because I lied to him that I was Isabeau—"

"Why wouldna you have lied?" the raider cut her off, something akin to sympathy in his dark eyes. "I'd say Conall's was a fortuitous blunder, aye?"

Lisette bobbed her head, then blurted, "I didn't lie about the cloak! Conall had wrapped me in it—but I never knew anything about the jewels. So much hatred...all of my life. I-I never meant any harm to Isabeau—"

"She meant grave harm tae you, Lady Campbell, but no longer. We'll let the fish have them."

Lisette heard a splash as Euan was dumped overboard, buckets of sea water poured upon the deck to wash away the blood.

More splashes followed as Euan's men leapt into the waves—including the two who had snatched her and Colin, all of them clearly frightened for their lives after what they'd seen. The raider only laughed, a cold, humorless sound that chilled Lisette as much as the grim look in his eyes.

"Aye, we'll let your husband serve his own justice upon them. Here he comes now, aye, and eager for that fight you spoke of."

Lisette gasped and followed the raider's gaze to where a fisherman's boat had been carried down to the beach and shoved into the water. Conall stood at the prow as a dozen men, Finlay among them, pulled hard on the oars.

The sword in Conall's hand glinting in the sun.

His face set with fury and his body stiff with tension when he saw the raider draw closer to Lisette, making her gasp. To her surprise, he had unwound his breacan of black-dyed wool and wrapped it snugly around her and Colin, chucking the boy under the chin with callused fingers.

"Forgive me, I should have done so earlier."

Lisette could but stare at him, his gruff apology the last thing she expected from him. He said no more, but strode back to the railing with his own sword in hand.

Who was this man that he could be so merciless one moment and then so kind in the next? Yet as soon as she hastened to join him, Colin thankfully not shivering half so much, she could see that the fierceness in his expression had returned.

Conall looked fearsome, too, as the boat drew closer, until a look of surprise overcame him, which made the raider chuckle under his breath.

"By God...*Gavin MacLachlan?*"

"Aye, Conall...and just know that your wife and son are safe and sound and their tormenters consigned tae the bottom of the ocean. Is it still your intent tae fight me, man, or will you come alongside and allow me tae lift them down tae you?"

"*Papa!*" interjected Colin, his tears ceased and his distress all but forgotten as he pointed at Conall, his blue eyes bright.

Lisette's tears weren't done, though, and she wept for joy when he drew close enough for her to see that moisture glimmered in his eyes, too.

Her heart hammering her throat. Her eagerness overwhelming her to feel his arms around her again...to feel him kiss her again.

"Say a good word for me," came the raider's low voice as the prow of Conall's boat scraped against the ship. "If I'd known an innocent lass would be wearing that cloak, I would have slain the whole accursed lot when we came upon their ship this morning and spared you and the boy much suffering—aye, your husband, too. Up with you now!"

He lifted her and Colin over the railing as if they

weighed nothing at all and handed them down to Conall, Lisette burying her tear-streaked face in his neck as Colin squealed and hugged his father.

"You've come up in the world, Campbell, from the runny-nosed whelp I once knew. A landed baron now—though you're still as reckless tae face me in that leaky vessel!"

"You were reckless, too, as I recall," Conall said with a wry retort, "and your cousin Finlay will vouch for it!"

Lisette glanced up in surprise to see a smile flash across the raider's face as he acknowledged his kinsman with a nod, but then he grew grim again as he gestured to the rocking vessel.

"Mayhap you might want tae keep MacCulloch's ship? I've no use for it—"

"*Burn it.*"

Lisette shivered at the harshness in Conall's voice, such gratitude flooding her that these two formidable warriors hadn't come to blows.

As he used his sword to push off from the ship, she looked up, wanting to thank the raider—*non*, Gavin—but he had disappeared beyond the railing.

The sound of chopping filled the air as ropes were cut, the two ships already drifting apart as Conall settled her and Colin on the floor of the boat with his arms like a protective shield around them.

Yet a few moments later, Gavin reappeared at the railing holding something in his hand.

"Catch, Conall! A wedding gift—though it's only half of the sultan's treasure. I'm not a fool!"

Conall did, snagging a small cloth bag tied with a strip of leather that Gavin had tossed high into the air. "Sultan's treasure?" he echoed, glancing at Lisette.

"I'll tell you all, husband," she murmured, but the crackling of flames drew her gaze back to the ship.

Black smoke spiraled upward from the doomed

vessel as a blood red sail was unfurled on the other ship and billowed in the wind.

Gavin's ship, Lisette sending a prayer for him heavenward though she didn't know where he was bound or what might have happened to him to choose the perilous life of a raider.

Not a devil at all...but an unforeseen avenging angel who had restored her family, her fingers entwining with Conall's as he leaned over to kiss her.

CHAPTER 22

"Forgive me, lass...*forgive me*."

As Conall pulled her close in their bed to hug her fiercely, Lisette didn't know what else she could say to him that she hadn't said for the past week.

Each morning had been the same, his apology the first thing he said to her when he felt her stirring from sleep.

He blamed himself still for what had happened to her and Colin, especially that he hadn't questioned the presence of the priest that had accompanied them to their new home.

Father Philip with his pale blue eyes and over-inquisitive manner and strange interest in the cloak she wore, and who as it turned out hadn't been a priest at all but pretending to be one. A similar ruse that Conall had employed only weeks ago in Dumfries!

All of this had been discovered after a messenger had been sent to Cameron and Aislinn with the jarring news of Lisette and Colin's ordeal.

Outraged and with the two blaming themselves as well, they had queried every servant and discovered a tenant farmer had been seen speaking near the kitchen with the priest and the serving maid—the man con-

206

fessing the entire scheme after he had been dragged before them.

The three conspirators sent there by Euan MacCulloch, who had sailed north with Isabeau aboard the ship that Gavin had set afire...

Lisette shuddered at the memory of her half-sister's blazing eyes when she had tried to shove her and Colin over the railing. At once Conall drew back to look at her, his fingers caressing a dark tendril from her face.

"Lisette?"

"She hated me so—ah, God, how will we ever move beyond what happened, with you still so tormented? It's done and past, Conall! I don't blame you at all and never would, but when will you forgive yourself?"

Tears had filled her eyes and she saw moisture in Conall's, too, which made her throw her arms around him to hug him tightly.

"I'm here with you and safe," she whispered fervently against his ear. "Our sweet Colin is safe, too."

"Aye, but if anything had happened tae you..."

Now Conall shuddered against her, her courageous and fierce warrior so vulnerable at that moment, Lisette thought her heart might break. All she could do was to hold him and kiss his damp cheek even as he turned his head to find her lips...his impassioned kiss taking her breath away.

She could feel the tension easing from his body as if convinced—at last!—that he must forgive himself just as she had pleaded with him.

Just as she must forgive Isabeau, for how else would she ever be free of painful memories Lisette only wanted to forget?

Heaven had blessed her with all she had ever hoped for—the miracle of love so profound and deep that she trembled in Conall's arms, murmuring, "*Je t'aime...je t'aime!*" against his lips.

"*J-Je t'aime*, lass," he answered her, his French awkward with his Highland burr no matter how heartfelt, which made her draw back from him, giggling.

Conall laughed, too, as she pressed her hands to the sides of his face to look into his eyes.

Joy brimming in those deep blue depths that matched her own as she felt his arms tighten around her.

A lusty darkening in his gaze that made her shiver with anticipation, though an impatient knocking on the door made Conall groan.

Colin burst in wearing his little nightshirt, Bonni hard upon his heels, the woman thankfully mended after what she had suffered—another blessing!

"Forgive me, Laird...Lady Campbell!" she cried, the boy's gleeful laughter echoing around the room as he clambered with amazing agility upon the bed.

"Mayhap three nursemaids, husband?" Lisette said with fresh giggles herself, Colin jumping up and down and brandishing a wooden horse as if he held a sword.

"Papa, look, I'm a raider like the devil of the seas!"

"You're soon tae be a sopping wet raider once I get you in your bath," Bonni said with a firm tone that made Colin stop his bouncing and leap into the nurse-maid's outstretched arms.

Yet she laughed, too, and hustled with him out of the room and shut the door behind them, while Conall groaned again and collapsed upon the bed to throw a pillow over his face.

"God help us, is this what we have in store? Our own raider in the family?" came his muffled voice, which made Lisette push away the pillow and snuggle into his arms.

"Kiss me, husband."

Conall did, chuckling against her lips while Lisette felt her heart full to bursting.

With gratitude for Gavin MacLachlan, wherever his ship had taken him...and with love brimming over for her handsome Highland warrior as she kissed Conall back.

A gold ring set with a perfectly rounded pearl, placed by him upon her finger, that she had thought she would never see again.

Sewn into the hem of the cloak she had worn without knowing her father's precious gift had been with her all along...

ALSO BY MIRIAM MINGER

Romance from sweet to sensual and historical to contemporary, you're sure to find stories to love!

Warriors of the Highlands

My Highland Warrior

My Highland Protector

My Highland Captor

My Highland Raider

My Highland Champion

THE MAN OF MY DREAMS

Regency Historical Romance

Secrets of Midnight

My Runaway Heart

My Forbidden Duchess

Kissed At Twilight

My Fugitive Prince

THE O'BYRNE BRIDES

Irish Medieval Historical Romance

Wild Angel

Wild Roses

Wild Moonlight

On A Wild Winter's Night

CAPTIVE BRIDES

Medieval Historical Romance

Twin Passions

Captive Rose

The Pagan's Prize

DANGEROUS MASQUERADE
18th Century Historical Romance

The Brigand Bride

The Impostor Bride

ROMANTIC SUSPENSE

Operation Hero

INSPIRATIONAL ROMANTIC SUSPENSE

Operation Rescue

TO LOVE A BILLIONAIRE
Steamy Contemporary Romance with an Historical Romance Story within a Story

The Maiden and the Billionaire

The Governess and the Billionaire

The Pirate Queen and the Billionaire

The Highland Bride and the Billionaire

WALKER CREEK BRIDES
Sweet Western Historical Romance

Kari

Ingrid

Lily

Pearl

Sage

Anita

ABOUT THE AUTHOR

Miriam Minger is the bestselling author of sweet to sensual historical romance that sweeps you from Viking times to Regency England to the American West. Miriam is also the author of contemporary romance, romantic suspense, inspirational romance, and children's books. She is the winner of several Romantic Times Reviewer's Choice Awards—including Best Medieval Historical Romance of the Year for The Pagan's Prize—and a two-time RITA Award Finalist for The Brigand Bride and Captive Rose.

Miriam loves to create stories that make you live and breathe the adventure, laugh and cry, and that touch your heart.

For a complete listing of books as well as excerpts and news about upcoming releases, and to connect with Miriam:

Visit Miriam's Website
Subscribe to Miriam's Newsletter